## About the Author

Isabelle Howe was born in 1960, raised in West Sussex and has lived there for most of her life. She is a successful mother and homemaker, raising her children and grandchildren, she has worked in this diverse world as a Revenue Accounts Clerk for an airline, a Pagan Chaplain for prisons, a Foster Parent, she has even been a Dinner Lady in a school. This is the first of many books she intends to write. She enjoys Yoga, growing organic food, and has more than fifty pairs of shoes (but it isn't a fetish!)

# Save Me

**Isabelle Howe**

# Save Me

Olympia Publishers
*London*

**www.olympiapublishers.com**
OLYMPIA PAPERBACK EDITION

A CIP catalogue record for this title is
available from the British Library.

ISBN: 978-1-78830-856-4

This is a work of fiction.
Names, characters, places and incidents originate from the writer's
imagination. Any resemblance to actual persons, living or dead, is
purely coincidental.

First Published in 2020

Olympia Publishers
Tallis House
2 Tallis Street
London
EC4Y 0AB

Printed in Great Britain

# Dedication

To my family who believed in me, and those who didn't, don't matter. And to Dawn Baker, without whom I would never have tried.

# Acknowledgements

Thanks for the opportunity.

# Chapter One
## The proposition

As she lay in her bed tossing and turning with the lucid dreams running through her head, she heard a voice in the darkness "Wake up," it said again and again. "Wake up Faith." She sat up with a start, looking around her room. Nothing. Her heart raced, her mouth was dry and panic set in. The air in her room became chilled, Faith reached for her robe, as she covered herself, she looked at her husband asleep next to her — it wasn't his voice. Again, the voice spoke, "Don't be alarmed, I mean no harm," still she couldn't see who was speaking.

"Where are you?" she said quietly as not to wake her husband, "Who are you?"

The voice spoke again, "I need your help," it said. In the corner of her eye she saw a movement in the shadows of the light from the landing that was shining under the door, the shadow moved forward into view. It was a woman, a very small woman, dressed in a long black robe, her hair was a deep shade of purple, her skin was pale but her lips were a deep red and she had no shoes on, her feet were petite. Faith got out of bed, "Am I dreaming?"

"No, I'm here to ask for your help to save someone, I will show you," she said. Faith quietly opened the bedroom door.

"Come with me," she said to the small apparition they went downstairs to the lounge, Faith felt the cold air as they moved. "You're not a ghost, are you?" she asked

"I think I'm just here," the woman said, "but I have been many things before now, but now I come to ask you to do something for me, save a life and change a life," she said.

"What do you mean?" Faith said puzzled, "Whose life?"

"Someone who wasn't supposed to die when he did, or the way he did," the woman said.

"How can I do anything if he is already dead?" she whispered.

"Don't worry about noise," the woman said, "no one can hear us. I am going to send you back in time to where he was healthy and happy — you need to warn him of what is to come, he made a mistake that changed his life forever, he was in love and happy, but doubt crept in. He changed; he became distant and started thinking thoughts that destroyed the relationship with the woman he loved, and then he went down the wrong path to his destruction."

"How can I warn him? He has free will; I can't tell him he's on the wrong path, do you know the mess I've made of my life?"

"Yes, I know everything about you, Faith, that's exactly why you can do this, you know how he feels, he never stopped loving her and she loved him. You have always wondered who you were and why things happened to you, now I can help you understand, you were meant for other things. All you ever wanted was a family that loved you, and to the most part you succeeded, but you have never truly been in love — people have tried to love you, but you have never loved anyone the way you wanted to," the apparition said.

"What the hell is love anyway," Faith said bitterly.

"Someone who loves you unconditionally even if you make mistakes and aren't perfect, even when you are not that lovable and at your worst. They still pick you up and help you make sense of life, fix you, make you see what they see in you, change the way you think about yourself, the doubts you have of your worth, someone who can't function without you in their life, love your children as you do, and understand why you love the way you do — someone who sees you in your entirety," she said.

"There is no such person," Faith snapped.

"Yes, there is, someone who has made as much of his life as he can but has also never felt the pang and the angst of true love, someone who is the fire to your water."

"What does that mean?" Faith said

"It means he is a fire sign and you know you are a water sign," the woman said.

"Yes, I see," said Faith.

"Someone who would never hurt you mentally or physically, loves music and isn't afraid to live. Someone who changes along with you, evolves, who grows with every mistake made. Life is not fool-proof, Faith, but you will meet this person," she said.

"And how is this going to change my life? I'm married to a good man; why would I leave him?" Faith said looking worried.

"You will understand soon, I promise. I'll send you back to live your life again," the woman said.

"I don't want to make different choices, my children won't be born!" Faith worried.

"Yes, they will, they might look different, you might even call them different names, and I can make them born on the same day if you want, but they will benefit from both parents who love them unconditionally," the woman said.

This made Faith think 'how hard it would be?' She thought for a long time, about how she always wanted to have all her children with one man, who loved them as much as she did, to have a normal life, not one of struggle and loss.

"I can swap mother for daughter if you would prefer?" the woman said. Faith looked at her, it was as though she read her mind.

"I have to think for a moment, do I have time?" Faith asked.

"Take all the time you want, Faith, you have to be sure."

"I have questions," Faith started, "can I have them in a different order, like all the boys then all the girls?"

"Yes, anything is possible," the woman replied.

"Can I have them closer together?"

"Yes," again she replied.

"Can I have blue or green eyes?"

The woman looked puzzled but agreed. "I suppose you want blond hair too?"

"No just a light brown is fine." Faith remembered how she used to have nice shiny brown hair. The woman nodded.

"All right," said Faith, "what do I do?"

The apparition gestured towards the next room, "Go through this door." Faith looked at her as though she had lost her marbles.

"That's my little living room," she said.

"It will take you to his bedroom."

"Are you mad?" Faith said in disbelief, "I'm not going in there, he would attack someone who just appeared in his bedroom in the dead of night."

The woman smiled. "He can't touch you, it would be like you aren't there."

"I don't want to give the guy a heart attack either," Faith said.

"His heart is strong," she said smiling.

"What do I say?" Faith asked.

"You will know him. Just speak kindly and he will just think it's a dream. He is alone tonight, his girlfriend is at her parents, but you must make him believe you, or he is doomed." The woman said seriously.

"I'm afraid," Faith said.

"Just think you are doing a good thing, he will be grateful."

"Who is he?" Faith asked.

"I can't say, just that you will know him," the woman said.

As Faith stepped through the door into a dark room, she bumped into a chair. Suddenly someone jumped up out of bed screaming, "Who are you? What are you doing here?"

Faith screamed, then they both screamed. The light came on and standing there, in his birthday suit, was the lead singer of Regent. Faith screamed again, "I'm so sorry," she said, "I didn't mean to scare you, I'm here to tell you…" she stopped. Then continued, "…well I don't know what I'm going to tell you, but it's important," she added. The young man stood silent for a second, then realised he didn't have anything on and grabbed the blanket from the bed, Faith turned away. "I'm sorry," she said half giggling. His cheeks turned red.

"How did you get in here?" he said firmly.

"I just walked in," Faith said, "I know it sounds crazy, but I have something to tell you, and you may not believe me, but please let me tell you," she said. He sat down on the bed and looked at the old woman who had just appeared in his bedroom.

"Are you real?" he said.

Faith thought for a moment, "I'm real but not in this time, well I am alive in this time but... not like this, erm, what is the date?"

"28th February," he said. My birthday Faith thought.

"What year?"

"1974, what year did you think it was?"

"2019," she replied, "well it is in my time, but I'm here now in your time," she said, hoping he believed her. Still, even she was feeling confused, "I'm just a kid in this time."

"Okay who are you?" he said looking at her as though she was mad.

"Faith," she said "Faith Tinsley, I'm not mad, I promise."

"So how did you get in here?" he seemed to be getting a little annoyed.

"I realise you are a bit put out by my appearance in here," she said, "wouldn't you rather put some clothes on?"

"Actually, I would rather you left and let me go back to sleep, that is if I'm even awake, and this isn't just a dream."

He went to touch her, but his hand wouldn't connect. He gasped. "Are you a ghost?" he said shakily.

"No, I'm not dead, well I hope not," she said touching her arm, "nope, I can touch my arm, but I don't think you can, which is lucky as you may hit me for being in here."

"I would never strike a lady," he said indignantly "especially one in pyjamas."

"Oh, that's comforting," she said, then realising she was actually in her pyjamas and grabbed the end of the blanket to cover herself up. "Can I please tell you what I have to tell you now?" she said hopefully. "I really don't think you would believe me, but I must try, you see you die, and I need to tell you how so you can avoid whatever kills you and we can all get on with living."

"When?" he shrieked. "Me die? How?"

"Well I'll tell you if you let me," she said. "I can't talk if you are hysterical, it doesn't happen yet, but you are on the path, you see. I have to get you off this path and onto the right one, so that it doesn't happen at all. It was such a shame, you were at the top and then you died, a loss to everyone really," she added.

"Really?" he said, "You mean we make it as a group or do we split up?"

"No, Regent was an amazing band, I mean not everyone's cup of tea, but you were very popular. Plus, your bandmates don't get over you dying, especially, oh what's his name your bassist?"

"Bob?" he said.

"Yes, that's him."

"Why, what happens to Bob?" he asked.

"Nothing. He played with some other band occasionally but gives it all up and sits at home with his wife and kids, I saw some pictures of him recently and he looked terrible," she said.

"That's a bit harsh isn't it? He looks OK for a twenty-three-year-old."

"Well he's sixty-eight in my time."

"Oh," he said. Then he got up and opened the bedroom door and ran to the bathroom, where he locked the door.

Faith sighed, 'Oh dear.' She followed him to the bathroom and stood outside for a moment. "Are you going to come out or did you just run away from me?"

He mumbled something to the effect of 'go away you, old bat'. She put her hand on the door, but it passed straight through. "Hmm," she thought, "that's strange." She walked through the door, what a strange feeling it was as she appeared in front of the young man just as he was putting on a bathrobe. "Oh," she said, "that's better isn't it? Are you coming out of here or do I have to sit on the side of the bath? Only my legs don't do so well when I'm standing for long periods," she said.

He nearly fainted. "Who are you?" he pleaded, "and why are you chasing me about?" he asked.

"Well I didn't run out of the bedroom like a little girl and lock myself in the loo, did I? And did you call me a bat? That wasn't very nice, was it? And I'm trying to help you too, how can I get you to believe me?" she said, "I know, ask me about music, something, anything."

"Okay what is the latest thing in your time?" he asked.

"I don't listen to new music, it's rubbish," she said then thought "Oh wait…" and Faith started to sing, "Tell me, something girl, are you happy in this modern world."

"Who is that?" he said.

"Lady Gaga, she's really good, Tony likes her."

"Who's Tony?"

"Isn't he your drummer?"

"Oh, he likes anything in a skirt," he said smirking.

"Well, that's not very nice either, is it?" she said trying not to laugh. "You can go and find the younger me. I remember I

18

wanted to go to a concert of yours at a theatre in London," she said.

"The Rainbow," he said.

"Yes, that's soon isn't it?" she said, "you could take me, tickets."

"What? Why would I do that?" he said astonished.

"It's my birthday, I would have loved to go to a concert for my birthday," she said smiling. "My name was Faith Palmer and I lived in West Sussex."

She grabbed a pen and a piece of paper from the hall table and scribbled her address down on it. As she looked at the pen in her hand, she wondered how she could pick that up but pass through a door, it was too baffling to think about.

"Why?" he said.

"Because then you will know I'm not lying, oh and if you do go, tell me to dump Martin, he's a jerk, and if I marry him I'll be a single parent of two by the age of seventeen," she said, and she thought that's probably what the woman meant, she may as well try not to go down the road she was on herself at the time, even though she would miss her darlings, she was promised to have them to this invisible lover she meets. I wonder who he's going to be she thought to herself.

"Excuse me," he said abruptly, "I thought you said your name was Faith Tinsley?"

"Well I'm married in my time," she said, thinking to herself the truth was that she was on her third marriage.

"Oh okay, what were you saying before that?" he asked.

"Oh yes," she said, "sorry, I was saying you are thinking you like some guy, but I'm here to say that it's a mistake and nothing good comes from it — if you stay with your girlfriend you won't die, I think. Well, I'm sure you won't get the thing that kills you, from her."

"What kills me," he said in horror.

"A horrible disease that attacks the immune system, there was no cure for it in your time, so you die from it. It kills a lot of people, no one knew how it was transmitted at first, but predominantly it's passed through bodily fluids such as saliva and blood, it's a bit like an STD, they eventually develop drugs to manage the symptoms but not in time for you, and your radio chum." I liked him she thought, so sad. "I don't know if I can come back a second time so I'm hoping you believe me and adjust your behaviour and stay with your girl, she really does love you and sticks by you right to the end. You leave your house to her and I think royalties too.

"But if you stay with her, she will give you children that eventually you will want, she calls her eldest son after you even though you broke her heart. She doesn't have a great love life either, and gets divorced twice, I'm told. I think no one comes close to you for her," Faith said, "Oh, and stay away from Munich, that scene isn't good for you. Those clubs in New York too, I understand you are very confused about yourself right now, but you don't need to experiment to find true love, especially when it's staring you right in the face, she really does love you, and I know you never love anyone as you love her, so why not just settle down?" Faith said.

"I like having fun," he said sulkily.

"No! No more fun!" she snapped, "Well at least till past the '90s — I think that's when they find the cure, or at least you won't die."

As he walked back to his bedroom, she followed him they sit on the bed, and he looks at her, "How old are you?" he asked.

"I'm sixty, why?" she said.

"Just wondered," he replied getting back into bed. She instinctively pulled the cover up to his chin and smiled.

"I hope you take heed of what I have told you, Ted, I remember when you died, everyone was sad, it seemed like the whole world was in mourning, I know it's hard, but you have wonderful friends in your band members, and you could have had a lovely family. No one should die that way, it's too horrible." She turned towards the wall and started to touch the place where she came into his room, but nothing happened, she couldn't leave.

"I've done what you asked," she said, "now let me through." He tried to ignore her, but she was getting louder, "Let me through," she demanded.

"Oh, for goodness sake can you be quieter," he said, "I'm trying to sleep, I'll let you out the front door."

"I'm not sure that would work," she replied, "I came in here, why can't I return?"

The women's voice appeared from the other side, "I don't think he believes you Faith, you should be able to walk through."

"What else can I tell him?" Faith said.

"Who is that," he said jumping out of his bed suddenly standing right behind her, "I heard a voice from the other side of the wall, there isn't a house in that direction no one can be there." Suddenly Faith fell through the wall and disappeared.

# Chapter Two
## The Meeting

Faith stood in her living room feeling very nervous, the woman was still there, "We must watch now," she said.

"Watch what?" Faith asked.

"What happens," the woman said.

"So I'll see myself and Ted?" Faith said.

"Yes, you can watch, but not communicate with them." the woman said.

"Who is the person I meet?" Faith asked.

"I cannot tell you, you just need to watch; hopefully, you have saved Ted's life, and your life will change for the better."

Faith sat on the cold leather sofa and wrapped herself in the comfortable throw she always kept there. She sat quietly and waited to see what would happen next, she hoped for the best.

Ted stood there looking at the place where Faith disappeared; he touched the wall it was solid. He got a static shock from the place she went through, he watched for a long time expecting her to return, but she didn't. He got back into bed and was soon asleep. He woke in the morning feeling groggy, his hand was still tingling from the static shock from the night before, and he felt as though he had been on the town all night, remembering the crazy dream he had. On his way to the bathroom he noticed the paper Faith had written her address on, he sat on the side of the bath reading it and rereading it, 'It must have been true or how did this get here,' he thought. He put the paper safely in his jacket pocket and went back to the bathroom where he turned the shower on and stepped under the warm water. It was comforting as he mulled the information Faith had given him through his head. Over and over he said to himself, "I don't want to die," as he washed himself. He dressed in a daze and left his flat without eating, he didn't even have a cup of tea, he put his jacket on as he descended the stairs where he bumped into Tony, the drummer in his band.

"What's wrong with you? You look terrible." he said laughing.

"I'm going to die," he said, looking his friend straight in the eyes.

"What? When? Are you ill?" Tony asked.

"No, I'm not ill now, but I'm going to die if I don't calm down and stop partying like I do," Ted said.

"Oh okay, yes, I did say to you it's all getting a bit too much, Pete and Bob don't even go to the parties any more, since they settled down, and I'm getting fed up with the same girls crashing the parties, all they want is to get laid, not that I'm complaining, but it does get a little boring, and I've been to the clinic more times than I can count!" Tony said.

"I'm going to get married." Ted announced.

"Are you? Does she know?" Tony said with a smirk on his face.

"No, but I'm going to tell her when she gets back tonight." Ted said as Tony followed him out of the building. The sun was shining, but there was a chill in the air.

"Where are we going? The studio is that way," Tony said.

"Oh, I'm going to the train station," Ted said.

"Why?" Tony asked.

"I'm going to find someone, and you're coming with me, I have something to do," Ted said.

"Whose ticket is that you are holding?" Tony asked, "I thought you were giving that to your sister."

"Yes," Ted replied, "I mean no, she doesn't want it she has a date that night, so its spare."

As they waited for the train, Ted bought a birthday card, and put the ticket inside and while they were on the train Ted wrote inside the card and explains to Tony what happened the night before.

"It was just a dream Ted, it can't actually be true", Tony said.

"How did this appear on my hall table then?" he said waving the paper with Faith's address on it in front of Tony's face, "this is not my writing. I'll know when we arrive at this address won't I."

"I think you're mad." Tony said, "but I'm intrigued. What if this Faith girl really exists, and she is going with a guy Martin, are you going to wig out or stay cool, cos if she exists, she is a child, and you will scare her."

"What am I going to say, 'hi I'm Ted and you came to me in a dream when you are sixty years old and told me to say dump Martin, cos he's no good for you.'" They sat and looked at each other, then burst out laughing,

"It's crazy!" Tony said "it can't be true."

"Well we will see," Ted said, "we are at our stop now."

They got off the train and went outside, the taxi rank was outside the station, they looked around, it was greener than London, with a big field in front of the station.

"Taxi mate?" said a voice from the booth.

"Oh yes." they said in unison. They sat in the cab, Ted gave the taxi driver the address and the cab took off at a steady pace. Ted and Tony didn't say a word during the seven-minute journey, they just took in the tree-lined streets of identical houses in rows after rows and parks, they pass a couple of schools and there was noise of children playing in the playground. The cab stopped.

"Two pounds please" the taxi driver said, they parted with the cash and got out. This street was just like any other council estate street, the cab drove off and they stood on the curb looking around.

"What's the number?" Tony asked as they look around.

"Nineteen." Ted said, they look at the closest house.

"Okay this is one-hundred and one." Tony said. They started to walk, as the numbers decreased.

"Seventy-five, keep walking," the road turned around a corner "fifty-two," they walked further down the road until they came to the last row "twenty-five, twenty-three, twenty-one, here it is nineteen." Ted said. Nervously, they opened the wooden gate.

"The hedge could do with a trim." Tony said.

Ted looked at him "What?"

"The hedge." he said again.

Ted looked at him and pulled a face, "So, it's not your hedge." he said.

"No, I don't have a garden," Tony said laughing. Suddenly a woman appeared putting a milk bottle on the doorstep.

"Mind my hydrangea," she said sharply.

"Oh sorry," they both said, stepping away from the small bush by the front door. There in front of them stood a small framed woman with jet black hair and a slight tan,

"Can I help you?" she said in a well-spoken voice.

Ted spoke first, "We are looking for Faith Palmer?"

"She isn't in," the woman said, "she was supposed to be back by now, but she isn't, probably with that boy she's seeing." They looked at each other and Ted felt a jolt in his stomach,

"I don't feel very well," he said to Tony.

"You can come in and wait if you want, I've just made a pot of tea."

"Oh, that would be lovely, I haven't had one all day. By chance is the boy Martin?" Ted said.

"Yes, that's him," the woman said, "awful boy, but she won't stop seeing him." They sat at a table in a small dining room as the woman set some cups and saucers on the table, there was a thick table cloth and a fresh, clean cotton cloth over the top.

"I take it you are Faith's mother," Ted said as he watched her pouring his tea through a strainer.

"Yes, Meg is my name. Milk?"

"Yes, please," he said.

"Help yourself to sugar," she said, as she poured Tony a cup, "and who are you?"

"Oh sorry, I'm Ted and this is Tony, we are musicians, that's a nice piano you have there."

"Oh yes I do like to tinkle the ivory's occasionally."

"Yes, I do too." agreed Ted.

"I'm a drummer," Tony said with a smile.

"Oh, really and how do you know my daughter?"

"That's a bit complicated, someone I met last night knows her very well and asked me to tell her to stop seeing that Martin fellow, so here I am," he said looking at Faith's mother to see if she believed him, "I promised you see," he said hopefully.

"Really, who is that?" she asked.

"Oh, erm a teacher of hers," he lied.

"That must have been Mrs Green, she tried to tell her to stop seeing him a few months ago, as I had told her what was going on and had said she wasn't to see him, but Faith doesn't do a thing I tell her lately." she said.

"Really? A bit headstrong then?" Tony said.

"Not usually, but over this boy, she is adamant he's the one she's going to marry."

"No!" Ted said a little louder than he meant to, "she can't marry him, he's not a good match for her, they are far too young even to be thinking about marriage, don't you think?" he said looking at Faith's mother.

"I'm sure it would be a huge mistake, but she will learn I'm sure." her mother said.

"But surely you wouldn't want her to make this mistake," Tony said quizzically.

"Of course not, but if she married him, she would learn by her mistakes," she replied. Just then the door banged. Someone ran up the stairs, and suddenly music came blaring out as the woman went to the bottom of the stairs, she called out, "Faith there's someone here to see you." The music stopped. Faith came down the stairs, she came through the door and stopped in her tracks, staring at the two men sitting at her dining table drinking tea.

"Erm hello," she said in disbelief, "what are you doing here?"

Ted looked at Tony and spoke first, "You know who we are?" Faith nodded dumbly, "Oh good." Ted said. "We have been asked to have a word with you."

"About what?" she asked.

"Oh, and happy birthday for yesterday." Ted said as he gave her the card, she opened it and blushed,

"For me?" she gushed, "how did you know it was my birthday," she said. "This is just what I wanted," she said looking at the ticket.

"Just tell the man at the front door I gave you this, and he will put you somewhere safer as it gets a bit squashed in the crowd." he said. Faith looked at her mother to make sure this was okay for her to go to, her mother nodded.

"I suppose you can go," she said.

"Well we need to talk with you, Faith."

"It's important," they both said.

"Can we go for a walk?" Ted asked.

"There's a park down the street, we could go there if you want," she said. They got up and thanked Faith's mother for the tea, and left the house. They slowly walked down to the playing fields at the corner of the street. The park was empty, so they walked to the swings, and each sat on one.

"Well," she said smiling for the first time. The sun made her hair look like deep gold and her skin was glowing, "what do you need to talk to me about?" she said.

Tony looked at the girl and spoke first, "how old are you, Faith?"

"Fifteen and you?" she replied.

"Erm," he said "I'm older," then smiled awkwardly.

Ted laughed, "That's not the point, how old we are, we are older than you, and we know what you are up to Faith."

She looked at them, "What do you mean what am I up to?"

"That boy you are seeing, you are way too young to be doing, well, you know what, with him." Ted said.

Faith laughed out loud, "What do you think I'm doing with that boy?"

Tony jumped in then, "You know what you have been doing with him, I hope you are taking precautions?"

Faith laughed again, "What if I'm not?"

"Well," said Ted, "that's silly isn't it." Faith had a wicked look on her face by this time.

"I don't feel silly," she said, "and neither does he, but we do take precautions sometimes," she said.

Tony got a little more serious now, he said, "What would you do if you got pregnant?"

She looked him straight in the eyes, "I would have a baby," she said seriously, "that's what happens when you get pregnant."

"You are so young, Faith why would you do that to yourself?" Ted said looking concerned. She suddenly looked very old and very serious,

"I will be happy" she said.

"But he will leave you and by the time he does you will have two children to raise by yourself," Ted interrupted.

"You don't know that!" she said sharply.

"Actually, I do know that" Ted said looking sad. He looked at the young girl remembering the look on the older Faith's face. She wasn't happy. Still, he couldn't tell the young girl that she had told him what happens to her.

"He won't leave me, he loves me," she said.

"He isn't capable of that emotion," Tony said softly, putting his hand on hers, "I know you think he loves you and he probably does, in his way, but it's a completely different feeling having a child to take care of. Does he have a job?"

"No, we are still at school," she said.

"How old is he?" Ted said.

"Nearly sixteen" she answered.

"So how are you going to support a child?" he said.

"I'm not pregnant now," she said, "I would wait 'till he left school and got a job," she said.

"Why?" Tony asked.

"I want a family," she said.

"Don't you have one?" asked Tony.

"Yes, but I want my own family, no one sees me," she said, looking very sad.

"But they will," Ted said.

"I'm not important to anyone, just Martin," she said.

"Yes, but if you stopped having sex with him would he still love you?" Ted said, "try it, see if it makes a difference."

"People should see you," Tony said "you are beautiful, why don't you try your hand at modelling."

"Modelling?" she said, "No but don't you need a portfolio? I don't even have a camera." she mumbled.

"I know someone who will take pictures of you," Tony said brightly, "she was at university with me, her name is

Sophie, I'll ask her, then I'll let you know okay? But please stop seeing this boy," he said.

"Or at least stop having sex with him." Ted interjected.

"I don't know, I'm not that pretty," Faith said "aren't you supposed to be thin and pretty to be a model?"

"No," Tony said, "you could be a catalogue model, you know, wear the clothes that people buy. Try it you may like it." he said laughing, "at least if you have a kid you will be able to buy it stuff."

Faith thought for a while and nodded, "okay, I'll give it a try"

"... and you will stop seeing that boy?" Ted asked hopefully.

"Maybe," she said, "I'm not going to promise, but I will stop sleeping with him, just to test your theory," she said seriously.

"Good," Ted said tapping her hand, "well I think we need to get back to work or the others will wonder where we are,"

Faith walked the short distance to the station with Ted and Tony, talking about music and life, as she waved them off on the train. They watched her as the train left the station, they looked at each other,

"What do you think?" Ted said.

"I don't know what to think" Tony said, "she's a stunner isn't she?"

"I'm not talking about the girl!" Ted said.

"Well I am," Tony said, laughing.

"I mean what do you think about last night?"

"Oh," Tony said, not paying attention, "it must be true."

Ted finally said, "yes."

Tony replied, "I hope she stops having you know what with that guy, it would be a shame if she were to go down that route."

"Yes, it would be a waste, but what about me?" Ted said.

"Ted," Tony said abruptly, "just do as she told you and it won't happen, get married, don't cheat, have loads of kids and be happy. The band is doing well, isn't it?"

"Yes, and it will get better, Faith told me." Ted said.

Suddenly Tony looked at Ted, "What was she like, you know, the old Faith?"

Ted looked out of the train window then said, "She had a sadness in her eyes I can't explain, but I can see the young Faith in her, she is still beautiful," Ted said. Tony thought for a while, as he looked out of the window of the train. They got back to London by midday and got to the studio. Tony phoned his friend Sophie and asked her to photograph Faith, she agreed,

"I'm not promising she will be a model," Sophie said, "I have a few connections with agents, but you know how you are with girls Tony, they are not always as pretty as you think they are."

He laughed, "okay, when are you free?"

"I'm away for a few weeks, but how about 23rd March? That's a Saturday."

"Yes, that's fine, I'll let her know," he said, "and thank you Sophie, I know things didn't end well for us, but you are a good friend."

"Yeah, yeah," she said jokingly, "actually I'm seeing a great guy now, and I'm happy for the first time in a long time, so thank you," she said laughing. He hung up the phone, then made his way down to the studio where there was an argument going on, as usual.

"No, no, it's just not right," Ted was saying, "and if you don't jump in on time, how is it going to be right?"

"Well now Tony's here I can get into it faster, as I just can't get the timing right," Bob said.

"Oh, glad you could make it Tony," they all said.

"Sorry," Tony apologised, "I was on the phone." He turned to Ted and smiled, "It's on"

"When?" Ted said.

"23rd March, it's a Saturday."

"Right, I better write that down or I'll forget," he said grabbing a pen from the desk, "you do know we are in Blackpool in two weeks, don't you?"

"Well that's perfect, it's only three nights away, and it's a week before the Rainbow" Tony said with a huge grin on his face. Ted looked worried.

"What's going on?" asked the other two men.

"Oh, nothing important." Tony said, "Let's get on with this." he said. They worked for the rest of the day on the songs they would be playing on tour.

# Chapter Three
## Studio

Faith was listening to music alone in her room. She spent a lot of time alone, she was mulling over what Ted and Tony had said to her. She had stopped having sex with Martin, and he stopped seeing her, so they were right about everything, she thought. The postman rattled the letterbox, she ran down the stairs to pick up the post, and found a letter addressed to herself. She opened it as she put the rest of the post on the coffee table, and returned to her room. The letter was from Tony, it read: 'Dear Faith, I have spoken to my friend Sophie, she has put aside Saturday 23$^{rd}$ March for you to come to her studio, can you make it? I'll wait for you at Victoria Station about ten a.m., best regards, your friend Tony.' There was a phone number at the bottom. She would have to go to the phone box to call him and let him know she could make it.

She sat on her bed looking at the letter, thinking what it would be like to be a model, she looked at her mother's catalogue and mimicked how the models stood and what hairstyles they wore. She had always taken good care of her hair, her mother had always said it was her crowning glory, as she brushed her hair and put it on one side then the other. She had just finished making a top out of some old dress material and decided to wear that to the shoot, with cream trousers and her one pair of platformed shoes that her brother had bought her for her birthday. She asked her sister if she could borrow her leather coat on the day, she agreed — of course she didn't tell her where she was going.

On the morning of the shoot Faith spent an hour in the bath scrubbing herself and washing her hair, then drying it, and put on her best clothes. She looked in the mirror, then asked her sister for the tenth time, "Do I look nice?"

"Yes, for the tenth time, where are you going anyway?"

"Oh, just to town with my friends." she answered, hoping her sister believed her.

"You're not seeing Martin, are you?" she said pointedly.

"I'm not going out with him any more, I told you that!" Faith snapped. Her sister thought she must have met someone else but didn't comment further. Faith looked once more in the mirror, then left the house it was eight thirty. It looked like it was going to rain, so she went back to get her umbrella, Faith hated to be late for anything. As she bought her train ticket, she looked at the timetable, 'oh good the train is due', she thought. As she sat on the bench and waited for the train, she had an awful feeling someone was watching her, she looked around but didn't see anyone. As the train came to a stop at the platform, Faith entered the first compartment, it was empty, she was glad as she hated sitting amongst strangers, but she wasn't alone for long. A man sat down opposite her, he looked a bit scruffy and smelled of tobacco. He smiled, she tried to ignore him, he tried to talk to her, she felt even more uncomfortable. When she didn't answer him, he got up and left the compartment, mumbling to himself about rude teenagers. Luckily the train was pulling into Victoria, she got off the train, and looked around. She couldn't see Tony, so she walked over to the notice boards, looking at the timetable. She was early so she sat on a bench to wait, hoping Tony hadn't forgotten her. Suddenly, someone plonked down beside her and made her jump.

"I'm so sorry I'm late." came a familiar voice as he took the hood from his head.

"You scared me!" she said holding her throat.

He laughed, "Come on or we will be late." He took her hand and pulled her from the bench, she tried to keep up as he strode towards the underground. The train stopped in front of them, and they jumped on and sat down. A couple of stops later they got off, "It's just around here," he said smiling, as they went up the stairs, "Are you excited?"

"I don't quite know how I'm feeling right now, I haven't been to London by myself."

"You're not by yourself, you're with me, I won't let anything happen to you." he said softly, holding her hand. They came to a large terrace of houses, four or five floors high. They went up the front stairs and he rang the doorbell, looking at Faith smiling. A young woman opened it, "Is Sophie here?" he asked.

"Just up those stairs." she gestured, shutting the door behind them.

They went up the stairs to see an open room with sofas and furry rugs everywhere. There was a big white screen up at the window with some spot-lights pointing at the floor, there was a stool in the centre.

"Take a seat, I'll be with you in a mo," came a voice from behind a door in the corner of the room. Tony sat down and pulled Faith with him, she fell on top of his legs trying not to laugh.

She nudged him, "budge over!" she said with a smile.

"Oh okay, I see what you are saying Tony," said a tall woman coming out of what looked like a cupboard, she was taking off some rubber gloves, "yes very pretty."

Faith looked behind her and realised she was talking about her, she blushed slightly, and got up to shake the woman's hand. "Faith." she said politely as she shook the woman's hand.

"I'm Sophie, can you take off your coat and sit on the stool for me please," she said stiffly. Faith took off her coat and threw it over Tony's head looking wickedly at him. Tony smiled and sat back to watch, "Oh no you don't." Sophie said, "I need you as a prop."

"What?" Tony started to say, but the look on Sophie's face stopped him saying anything else.

"You can stand behind her as though you are supporting her." Tony did as he was told as he didn't want to upset Sophie or she may not do the shoot. He knew she was very good at what she did. But very bossy too. "Lean back into him." Sophie said. Faith leant back against Tony's chest, "now look down."

As Sophie clicked away with her camera, all Tony could smell was the scent of Faith's hair, she smelled so good,

"Okay, Tony take the shirt off, and Faith put your head on his chest," Sophie said, with a wicked look on her face. Faith turned a bright shade of red but did what she was instructed. Tony gently put his hands on her head as her cheek brushed his chest. He smelled clean and manly, she inhaled him closing her eyes, as Sophie clicked away.

"Look up, like you're asking him a question," Sophie said. Faith did as she was told, Tony looked her straight in the eyes and she felt her stomach turn. He was so nice she thought to herself.

"Good, good," Sophie said. Tony looked into Faith's face and smiled. Faith couldn't breathe, she couldn't hide how she felt at that moment, his eyes were a beautiful shade of blue/grey. He held her so softly, she noticed he was getting goose bumps, yet it wasn't cold in the studio. Suddenly Sophie said, "That's it, I've got all I need for now."

The jolt made Tony jump, "Erm yes, very good." he choked moving away from Faith. As he did so, she nearly fell off the stool, "oh sorry," he said, as he grabbed her arm.

She laughed. "That could have been bad," she said, as he saved her from crashing into the lights.

"I think I know who would be interested in these," Sophie said, pretending not to see them almost destroy her studio, "but I won't know for sure for a couple of weeks. How do I get in touch with you Faith?"

"I'll give you my address," she said, "do you have some paper?"

"No darling, I have to put this in my book, or I'll lose it. And if I lose your contact details, I'll have to contact Tony, and I don't really want to chase him around the country."

"I'm on tour for a few days too so I won't be around for a while either," he added, "I will be seeing you next week, however, as you will be coming to the show," he said smiling. "If you play your cards right you may get to the party after, that's if you want." he said looking at Faith.

"I would love to, but I don't know if I would be able to stay out that late." she said, as they put on their coats and got ready to leave the studio. Faith shook Sophie's hand again and thanked her, Tony winked at Sophie, and they descended the stairs to the front door

"Let's get some lunch now, I'm starving." he said as they left the studio. Sophie shook her head; she could see the chemistry between them immediately.

Around the corner was a small café where they had the most delicious sandwiches, and the cakes looked nice too. Tony ordered a ham and cheese and Faith had chicken salad with a pot of tea and a scone with strawberry jam and cream. After they had eaten Faith felt very bloated, Tony asked Faith what time she had to be home by,

"I have to be home by ten thirty." she said.

"Tonight?" he said.

"Yes." Faith nodded.

"Okay, do you want to see how we work?" He asked.

"What? Go to the studio with you?" she said, looking excited.

"Yes, Ted will be there by now, and the others, you can listen if you like."

Faith smiled. "I would love that," she said sweetly. He took her hand softly and led her back to the underground. Arriving at the studio, Faith sat on a stool in the control room with Bob and Ted while Tony played the drums. He looked so serious while he was playing. Pete played amazing riffs on his guitar.

Finally, it came time for Faith to go home, Tony took her back to the station and kissed her goodbye, "See you next weekend," he said "stay safe and be good."

"I will." she promised. She got on the train that took her home. As she sat on the train replaying the day happily, she thought about how he had held her hand and kissed her goodbye, she couldn't help thinking how much she liked Tony.

Older Faith sat watching in disbelief "Oh my god, I know what's happening!" she said with her hand over her mouth then she started to cry. "Why?" she said, "why him?"

The woman looked at her questioningly, "he is lovely and all," Faith started to say, "but he will destroy me! I will fall in love with him, and he will destroy me, and in turn our children, if we have any.

"Or even if it lasts that long" she said tearfully, "you said he would love me forever, and our children but why would he want to? He could have anyone."

The woman spoke softly, "Faith you must believe the fates have decided, that you will marry him and live a long and fulfilling life together."

"Oh yes, I'm sure…" Faith said, "…until he cheats and breaks my heart!"

"All relationships need feeding Faith, you know that."

"Yes, I do, but I can't share with the world."

"You won't have to, he won't respond the way you think he will. He will love you and feel secure in your love; he will know you love him for him, and not who he is."

"How will he know that?" Faith asked.

"Because you will show him, Faith, you have so much capacity to love," the woman said.

"I have never been in love; how do you know that?" Faith said waiting for the answer.

"The fates have decided this is what you should have had all these years. You have sacrificed for your family, always doing the right thing, now there are two of you sacrificing and doing the right thing together, you can be happy and secure in the knowledge that you are loved wholly, unconditionally, you

40

can be you and he can be him. You won't always see eye to eye, but you will support each other in your lives."

Faith calmly sat watching her life unfold before her eyes, she saw how he treated her, and thought maybe just maybe the fates were right.

The next day Tony went to the studio where he met a stern-looking Ted, "What's wrong?" he said.

"Are you mad" he said frowning at Tony.

"What?" Tony said looking innocent.

"She is a child." Ted said, "I know what you are thinking Tony, I've known you too long to think you are just being nice to her."

"I can't help it, Ted, I've never met someone like her before." Tony said as he sat on a chair.

"Well the press will destroy you, and us with you, if you pursue this, you know that don't you?" Ted said.

"Look we are on tour soon, we will be gone most of the year, I won't see her 'till the end of March, and then we will be gone, I'll be discreet, I'm not thinking of anything else I promise, I wouldn't do that, what do you take me for?" he said.

Ted looked at Tony with concern, "I do see what you see in her. She is lovely, but she has a year before you can see her. Promise you won't try to see her before. Tony?" Ted's eyes narrowed, "Tony are you listening?"

"I'm not a child Ted, don't talk to me like one." Tony said angrily.

"I know you are not a child, but she is," Ted said.

"You don't understand," Tony spat.

"Yes, I do," Ted said "I understand very well. But you must wait."

"I will wait, I've promised you, haven't I?" Tony said.

"Okay that's the end of it then." Ted said.

"Well I've invited her to the party after the Rainbow." Tony said.

"Why? She can't be there with all that debauchery!" Ted said.

"Oh my god Ted, she isn't innocent, she knows what happens at parties." Tony said.

"Well it had better not, that's all I have to say." Ted said and left the room. "I'll be back with coffee you want some?" he shouted from the hallway.

"Yes please," Tony said. And the argument was forgotten. Bob and Pete knew there had been a discussion but were ignorant of the topic, so they stayed out of it.

# Chapter Four
## The show

The next week went by fast, it was time for Faith to return to London this time for the much-awaited concert. Without much trouble she found her way to the venue and showed her ticket, telling the usher that Ted gave her the ticket and was expecting her. He took her to the front behind the barrier. As she took a seat, a man on the other side of the barrier tried to get her to let him in, "I'm sorry she said I can't."

"Oh, go on," he said, "I'll make it worth your while." Faith tried to ignore him but he started to shout at her menacingly.

As the venue started to fill up, suddenly a large man came up behind him and grabbed him, and took him out. Faith didn't know but Tony was watching her from behind the stage, he instructed the usher to take that guy out. Just as the lights went out, she sat wondering what was happening, when the music started, and suddenly the lights flashed and the concert had started. The crowd cheered, it was amazing, you could feel the atmosphere, it was crazy. Ted was leaping all around the stage dancing and singing, the music was out of this world. Faith couldn't believe her ears, she sang along with the songs she knew, but just listened to the ones she didn't know. The guitars and drums were making sounds she didn't even know was possible, and Ted's piano playing was amazing, he sang like nothing she had ever heard before, and too soon it was all over.

Faith sat there deflated for a while. She watched the crowd disappear through the doors at the back of the venue, then the usher appeared again and he asked her to follow him. He led her to the rooms behind the stage, then out to a waiting car. She got in and there, waiting for her, was Tony.

"Hey you," he said as she sat beside him, "sorry I'm all sweaty," he added as the car sped off as though someone was chasing them. Faith held on to her seat for dear life, as the car came to a halt they were at the back entrance of a hotel. Tony took her hand, he told her to run to the open door before anyone saw them. She ran as fast as she could through the door and into a lift. He pressed number two and the lift doors closed, he wrapped his arms around her and kissed her, she melted in his arms, "I missed you." he said.

"I missed you too," she responded. The doors opened and they walked to his room. As he opened his door, he told her he needed a shower but promised he wouldn't be long. As he undressed and went to the bathroom, she looked around the hotel room. There wasn't much to look at, a bed and a dresser and a wardrobe, she removed her shoes and sat on the bed, flicking through the channels of the tv. He was true to his word, he wasn't long, he came out of the bathroom all clean and he smelled so good. "You don't live here, do you?" she asked.

"God no, but it's convenient when we do a show, we stay close to the venues." She sat taking in the sight for a second, then he realised he needed to dress away from the young girl, he didn't want to get into more trouble than he was in letting her come to his room, Ted was going to kill him, but he couldn't hide his feelings for Faith and she was so receptive to him. Once he was dressed, he sat on the bed ready to go, he said, "I have to talk to you first, though I don't want you to be scared or shocked. Our parties are a bit wild."

"I can't stay long." she said, looking very sad, "I have to get back by midnight."

"That's okay, I'll drive you home, or rather I'll get the driver to take you home as I will probably be drunk." he said laughing, "and listen, I need to say this, I don't want you feeling hurt, you are too young to be with me, you know that don't you?"

"Yes." she said quietly, her heart sunk, waiting for the words to cut her into pieces.

"So we need to keep it quiet." he said, "I'll kiss you and we can cuddle, but only when we are alone, and when we are in public we are just friends. I can't do anything else. I can't risk my career or that of my band mates, on a scandal." he said.

"I understand" she said seriously, the excitement building in her stomach. She thought for a moment then said "Do you think it would be better if you took me home now then and you go to the party later, I really don't want to get you into trouble."

He smiled. "If that's what you think is best, okay I'll get the driver." He left the room, moments later he was back, he took her hand and they left. It was an hour's drive, Faith thought she was going to die, she wanted Tony so much, and she knew he wanted her as they kissed in the back of the car. Finally, the car came to a halt outside Faith's house, she kissed him once more and tearfully said goodbye. "I'll see you in July," he said, "that's when we are back in the country."

She nodded and touched his face and kissed him again, "Bye." she whispered as she left the car. He watched her enter her house, then signalled the driver to go back to the party.

Faith had never wanted someone like that before, she didn't know how she was going to keep herself busy while Tony was gone. She entered her house, it was dark, everyone had gone to bed. Faith went to her room and quietly undressed for bed, but she found sleep alluded her, all she could think of was Tony, and how he made her feel. Eventually she drifted off to sleep with a warm glow and a smile.

Tony got back to the party. As soon as he got there, he was surrounded by hot blooded women expecting him to make a fuss of them, but all he could manage was a weak hello and went to the bar to get a drink. Ted made his way over to him "Where have you been Tony? We've been waiting for you. Where's Faith?"

"I took her home, we thought it was best, under the circumstances."

Ted tapped his friend on the shoulder "It is best." he said, "is that it then? Are you seeing her when we get back in July?"

"Yes, I am," Tony said, "but I'm going to keep it under wraps, can't let anyone know."

Ted sighed, "I thought you would come to your senses, but I see I'm wrong again", Ted said sternly. "I'm having a small wedding for me and Kate in July, I want you to be best man, are you up for it?" asked Ted

"Yes sure, congratulations, can I bring Faith?" Tony said with renewed interest.

"Sure," Ted said "as long as you are happy."

"I am," Tony said "really happy, but for now, I'm going to get drunk."

Ted watched Tony all night, he didn't so much as kiss any of the women at the party,

"What's wrong darling?" came a voice from behind him, he turned to face his lovely Kate.

"I'm worried about him." He replied, as they both looked at Tony sitting on a bar stool chugging down beer.

"What's going on with him? He hasn't got anyone in his arms." Kate said, laughing softly.

"The one he wants in his arms right now, is way too young to be here. Still, he can't stop thinking about her."

"Oh, poor thing, that must be hell" she said cuddling up to Ted.

"I'm hoping he forgets about her for a while; honestly, if he goes for it, he could land himself in deep trouble and us too".

# Chapter Five
## The Agency

It was Monday morning. Faith's mother shouted at Faith to get up, there was a letter for her, and she was going to be late for school. Faith came down the stairs feeling very tired; she had been up half the night listening to music. She opened the letter, it was from Sophie, she had sent the pictures to all her agent friends and got so many replies she didn't know what to do, enclosed were copies of the pictures. Faith looked at them and smiled, they were really good. Tony looked so protective in them holding her. As she looked at them, she relived how she had felt that day.

"Who's that?" a voice came from behind her, her sister hadn't gone to work yet. Faith didn't want her to see how happy she was, as she had a habit of squashing all hope of a nice life for Faith, but it was too late. She had seen one of the pictures and saw there were more. Faith kept the best one back so her sister couldn't do anything to it, and handed the pile of pictures to her sister, "hm, you look nice." she said. Faith was surprised. "Who's the guy?"

"That's Tony, mum has met him, he was just posing with me." She would never tell her sister the truth, that she was undeniably in love with him, and she had spent Saturday night snogging him in the back of his car.

Her sister gave the pictures back and left for work, Faith looked at them again, then put them in her drawer under her underwear. She got some money and, on her way to school which she was over an hour late for, she phoned Sophie from the phone box at the end of her street.

"Hi Sophie, it's Faith," she started to say.

"Oh my god, thanks for getting back to me so fast," came Sophie's voice, "I don't know what to do, I tried to get hold of Tony but he's off doing his tour, and I didn't think you had a phone." Sophie said.

"I don't, I'm in a phone box." Faith said.

"Well I sent your pictures to a few of my friends in the business and they all want you to do modelling for them." Sophie said.

"I can't leave school yet," Faith said panic-stricken, "unless they will provide me with a tutor, and I haven't asked my mother yet." she said. "The holidays are coming up in April, I can come up then, but they will have to pay my travel."

"No Faith, you don't understand they are big model agencies, they would provide a car to pick you up every day, and give you a tutor, even have you stay in a hotel on location. You could go anywhere, Milan, Paris, New York, even Los Angeles."

Faith panicked again for a second, "I don't have a passport." she said.

"Don't worry about that," Sophie said, "they have people to get them fast, you could be in Italy by next week."

"I better ask my mother tonight then," Faith said, "I'll call you tomorrow."

"Okay" said Sophie.

"I'll come up on Saturday, we can go through the offers together." Faith said.

"Sounds good to me." Sophie said. They finished the call and Faith went to school, she was just in time for break and just slipped in the next lesson,

"Where have you been?" said her friends.

"I had an important phone call, but as far as you know, I have been in the loos puking all morning, that'll give them something to mull over."

They all laughed. "They will think you are pregnant", one of her friends said, "you haven't been going out with Martin for weeks, so they will think its him."

Faith laughed again "Oh well, it will give them something to gossip about. I might not be here much longer anyway, I have a modelling job to consider."

"Wow, where?" her friends said.

"I don't know yet, I only had the pictures done two weeks ago." she said.

One of her friends made a noise to imply she didn't believe her. Faith just looked at her. The friend backed down immediately then said "Oh yes, how did the gig go? Did you meet that guy?" she asked in a tone that again implied she didn't believe her.

"I might have," Faith said, "but if I did, I would never tell." Faith didn't care if no-one believed her; they would see when she doesn't go back to school.

It seemed like forever waiting for her mother to come through the door that night. Faith had cooked dinner, it was almost ready to dish up, and she was nervous about asking her mother. She was so unpredictable, one day she would let her go to London alone, and then she wouldn't let her out at all, she was very difficult to read. At last, she came through the door. "Oh, that smells good." she said.

"I just thought I'd cook to save you the trouble." Faith said looking very guilty.

"What have you done now Faith?" her mother snapped.

"Nothing, well almost nothing, I went to London a few weeks ago and had some pictures taken for a model agency, and they have now asked me to model for them."

"What kind of modelling Faith! Better not be naked." her mother said.

Faith immediately thought of Tony's bare chest against her cheek, "No, I was fully clothed at all times mum, I'm not comfortable taking my clothes off in front of people." she said.

"No, just that horrible boy Martin." her mother snapped.

"I haven't seen Martin for weeks, I promised I wouldn't." Faith said.

"Oh yes that's right you promised those two lovely men. I liked them they were decent, not at all common, must not have been from around here." her mother said.

"No, they live in London. Tony came with me to have the photos done."

"Did he now?" Her mother looked at her; she noticed immediately that Faith was blushing slightly, but said nothing more.

"But now they want me to model I need your permission." Faith said looking worried. "I thought they would say no, but they didn't," she said.

"All right, you can go." her mother said.

"I'm sure they will give you some paperwork to sign," Faith said.

"I'm sure they will. Let's eat before this all gets cold, I'm starved," her mother said.

Faith was so excited she thought she would burst, she wanted to talk to Tony so badly. Even though he had given her a breakdown of where he would be, she never seemed to be able to get hold of him, either he had just left or was asleep. He sent her postcards from where he had been but going to the stupid phone box was getting old. When I get some money, I'll put in a phone she thought.

Saturday came quickly and she climbed the train platform once again, it seemed like the train was so slow and when it finally got to the station Faith almost ran to the underground. She hardly noticed the fine weather, all she could think about was getting to Sophie's studio.

Finally, she was climbing the stairs and rang the bell, Sophie answered the door. "There you are." she said with a smile. "I've got all the paper work for you to fill out and permission slips for your mother to sign. I've spoken to the agent that is the best option right now, who pays the most, they are willing to have you here in London for the first few weeks to teach you, and have you join the other girls. You have to stay during the week and you can go home at the weekend.

"They have given you a retainer so you can buy some clothes and such, and a suitcase. they will sort your passport out, your mother just has to fill in this form, and you need your birth certificate too, they will do the rest. The place you will be staying is like a school so there are lessons available if you want."

"I think I should do some lessons to keep my mother happy," Faith said earnestly.

"Now here comes the money part," Sophie said, "first they have given you a list of clothing you must buy, and here's a thousand pounds," she said waving a wad of cash in her hand. "I can come with you if you want?" Sophie said. Faith looked at the money — she had never seen so much money, and this was hers. Sophie looked at Faith laughing, she was so dumbstruck she didn't answer for a good few minutes.

"No that's fine I can shop at home, when do they want me there?" she said in a daze.

"Two weeks from Monday." Sophie said looking at her diary.

"That's 22$^{nd}$ May." Faith said looking over her shoulder.

"Yes, that's right." Sophie said checking the dates off her calendar pinned to the wall, she turned to Faith "I need to have a visual reminder." Faith nodded, she took the envelope of cash and put it safely in her bag, and before she left, Sophie said, "If you need anything at all, just call me, won't you?"

Faith smiled "I will, thank you, Sophie." Then she left holding the paperwork in a folder.

Faith took Monday off school to go shopping. She looked at the list, there was an awful lot of things she had to buy. Still, she set to and gradually got everything making sure she matched colours and styles. She had never had the money to buy herself clothes on this scale, she had the babysitting job that helped her get some things, but this was bliss, she could buy the styles she liked, in fact, anything she wanted to buy she could. As she finished, she was confused as there was quite a lot of money left, so she went around to her bank and deposited a good amount and kept a little back for incidentals. She was glad she didn't have to babysit for her money now.

Tuesday, she went back to Sophie's studio and gave her all the signed forms. She was wearing some of her new clothes and looked good even though she did say so herself. Sophie liked her style, she introduced her to her friend Heather from the agency Faith was going to work for, she was terribly posh and looked so elegant.

"Oh yes, did I tell you?" Sophie said, "they have a new deal for you, after Italy you will be doing a TV advert with John Wayne. It's just a small part I'm sure you will be fine."

Heather said "I have a good feeling about you Faith."

Faith was speechless "wow" she kept on saying and "oh my god."

Sophie laughed, "It will be fine Faith."

"Yes, I'm sure it will." Faith said, "I'm sorry you must think me awfully ungrateful. I'm really excited but really scared at the same time." she said.

"I'm sure you are." Sophie said.

"That's quite normal," Heather interjected "but it won't take you long to get used to this way of life Faith. I'm sure you will be fine, but be prepared, you will grow up really fast. I'll give you some advice if you want it." she said. "You will be offered things that make you feel differently, either booze or drugs."

Faith looked horrified, "Why would I want to take drugs?" she asked.

"Well if you are feeling nervous someone might offer you a pill. This is a slippery slope, if you start you may not be able to stop. I've seen it happen to loads of people and it's not a pretty sight."

"I do drink," Faith said, "but I wouldn't drink if I had to work."

"That's good," Sophie said.

"But if you drink every day you may not be able to function properly without it." Heather said.

Faith sat down on the sofa. "You mean it's addictive?" she said.

"Yes, and you start to lose your looks and in turn you won't be offered jobs. Drink plenty of water and eat properly, and you will be fine. Stay away from drugs and drink okay." Heather said looking Faith in the eyes.

"I would hate to hear you lost the looks that you were given." Sophie said.

Faith got up. "I will stay away from drugs Sophie, I promise, and I'll only drink socially." she said in earnest.

"Good" Sophie said.

Faith shook Heather's hand and gave Sophie a hug. She left Sophie's feeling positive, she knew she wouldn't do those things, she wanted a good life and she didn't want anything to get in the way of that. She spent the rest of the day wandering around London looking at Buckingham Palace and some free art galleries. She thought about all the things she would be doing in the next couple of months and she was very excited. As she was sitting in a café drinking a cup of very expensive coffee, she mused about the life she wanted and wondered if she was ready for this. As she sipped her coffee, she thought about how happy she would be to go to America and Europe and wondered how many countries she would travel to. It scared her a little bit, it was getting late but Faith didn't want to go home, she was buzzing, and she loved looking around London, the fancy shops and cafés. Suddenly a voice rang out.

"Faith?" As she turned around, she saw Tony and his friends coming out of a bar. Ted wasn't with them.

"Tony, hi." she said smiling, "I've just been to Sophies, I thought you were away."

"We got back this morning. Pete is very ill, so we had to cut our tour short. Do you want to come back to my place? We are just going to rest a little."

Faith looked a little surprised, "I thought we decided it wasn't a good idea."

"Come on, one drink won't hurt, then I'll take you home." he said holding her hand. Faith wanted to so much, she had so much to tell him and didn't really want to go home right now, and even though she knew it would be a bad idea, she agreed. She couldn't help herself, with his disarming smile. He wouldn't do anything silly.

"One drink then." she said and went with him. His mates were already half cut and they didn't remember who she was, that was a relief as she didn't want someone to remind her who she was, and how old she was. But she needn't have worried Tony was as good as his word he called his driver to drive them home to Faith's house. They talked all the way how she was inundated with offers.

"I told you," he said, "are you excited to go to Italy?"

"Not really," she said, "I'm more excited to go to America and meet John Wayne."

"Wow, when is that happening?" he asked.

"Straight after Italy. I won't be there long as it's just a small advert, but at least I'll be working with my hero." she said.

Tony frowned. "I thought I was your hero," he laughed.

"No," she said, "you are something else, I can't even bring myself to say it out loud," she added quietly. He looked at her intensely. He could see she was thinking about something.

"Why so sad?" he said to her.

"I'm not sad." she said, "I'm happy, this is my happy face." and she grinned. They both laughed. "I'm just a little worried about going to Italy alone" she said. "I'll be in London for a few weeks then off to Italy for five days, then America."

"Where are you staying in London?" Tony asked.

"I have no idea, the agency uses different hotels."

Just as they were having this conversation the driver pulled up outside Faith's house, she suddenly felt so sad, she didn't want to leave Tony.

He held her chin softly and looked into her eyes, "It's all right Faith, it's just for now. One day I won't take you home, and you will be with me as often as you want, I promise." he said.

"Don't promise me things like that Tony." she whispered.

"Why, I mean it." he said louder than he meant to. "Sorry, I know it's hard but if it's meant to be, it will be. I'm waiting for you, I will be there anytime you need me, do you still have my phone number?" She nodded. "Don't lose it, will you, what are you doing tomorrow?" he said.

"I'm at school tomorrow. I have to give the paperwork to the headmistress so I can take time out of school." she explained.

"Okay, I'm at the studio all day. We are working on our next album, but I can get free at about six o'clock, I can pick you up at seven o'clock. We can go out for dinner and maybe a movie?" he said.

"Sounds nice, I'll see you tomorrow then." she said smiling and kissed him goodbye.

As she entered the house her mother was sitting in her usual place reading a book, but her sister was looking at her intently, "who was that you were kissing in that car Faith?"

Her mother sat up. "Kissing!" she said sternly.

"I just kissed his cheek," Faith said nonchalantly scowling at her sister.

"Didn't look like his cheek."

"Well it was, so there!" And with that Faith went to her room to get her things packed for London.

Her mother followed her upstairs, "What hotel are they putting you in Faith?" she tried to say over the music, that Faith instinctively put on every time she went to her room, "Can you turn that down for a moment, I'm trying to talk to you."

Faith turned her stereo down. "I'm not sure yet, they have a few hotels they use, it depends on where they have a room empty."

"Oh okay, let me know as soon as you know then, okay?" Her mother said.

"I would mum, but we don't have a phone." Faith said.

"You can call Sylvia, and she will tell me on Thursday," Sylvia was her mother's closest friend, "and don't forget to get the number." her mother shouted as she went back downstairs to her book.

"Okay I will." Faith said, as she turned the music up and carried on packing her case. As Faith finished, she lay on her bed dreaming about her and Tony together; she couldn't help but smile at the prospect of never going back home, did he mean she would live with him? She didn't care, she just lay there wondering what on earth he saw in her. He obviously did see something in her, or he wouldn't bother with her at all, he had girls lining up at his door, she fell asleep still wondering. But it invaded her, she dreamt he was shouting at her go away, he was saying, you silly little girl, and he was surrounded by beautiful women and they were all laughing at her. She woke up with a start tears flowing down her face, you stupid girl, of course, he doesn't want you, you are way too young for him! She told herself, she cried herself back to sleep.

As Tony got back to his flat, he was feeling tired but couldn't stop thinking about Faith; she was so young how could he be thinking of being with her? All common sense said that he was being very foolish. Still, all he could think of was how wonderful it would be. She always smelled of perfume even when she didn't have any on, so feminine, her skin was so soft and kissing her was more pleasurable than he had felt in a long time. He wondered how much she liked him, and what if she met someone else before she was of an age when it was decent for him to date her. But he didn't want to date her, he wanted her heart and soul.

Tony dialled Ted's number. It was late, but he needed to talk to someone who understood how he felt, and Ted had always known Tony's deepest desires. It rang, there was a muffled sound, then Ted's voice said sleepily, "This had better be important!"

"It is," Tony said, "I'm in crisis, I need your ear, just for a while."

"If it's about Faith," Ted said, "just don't try so hard and wait, you will get her, but beware of what you wish for Tony. She is young and inexperienced, take it very slowly teach her well, and you will be very happy I'm sure, but you mess with her, and you will ruin her for all other men and lose her."

Tony thought about how it would kill him to see her hurt. If it was him who caused her to hurt, he couldn't live with himself. He had a very honest relationship with Ted, he knew Ted meant what he said, they had grown up together, been bad boys together. Ted knew all the nitty-gritty, all the things Tony had done to and with women, some he was glad to have done, other things he wasn't so proud of. He knew what he was capable of doing, things he didn't want Faith to know about, but he also knew Ted would never betray his trust. He was in agony, he wanted Faith in his life and would shift heaven and earth to keep her happy. Still, the wait might be too much; Ted knew he had to do something, he needed Tony to focus on the band at least until they started to get decent money in, he thought if Tony could only focus on Faith, it would be disastrous for the band.

The next day Faith took her paperwork to the head of her school and had a little chat to her about what was going to happen with her education. She left feeling drained.

She bumped into some of her friends, they looked at Faith "You look nice" one of them said.

"Thanks," Faith replied "I'm off to London in a couple of days" she said looking at the friend who didn't believe Faith had this new opportunity.

"Oh, where are you staying, with that guy you met" she said looking down her nose at Faith.

"Of course I'm not, what do you take me for? I'm staying at the modelling school in Kensington." she said. "I probably won't see you guys for a long time, so bye." she said waving as she walked away.

They watched her walk down the street "I don't believe her, do you?" the girl said to the others.

"We don't know." they said shrugging their shoulders, "I'm sure we will find out when we see her in a magazine" they said as they walked back into the school.

Faith hadn't slept well the night before and was unsure if Tony would turn up that night, but she got ready anyway. At six o'clock there came a knock at the door, it was Tony he had got away early as he couldn't concentrate on anything while he had Faith on his mind. Her stomach churned when she saw him, he had a huge grin on his face,

"Hi." she whispered as she jumped into his arms, he kissed her and held her tight.

"Ready to go?" he asked.

"Always" she said smiling.

"Let's go." He said holding her hand as they walked to town. He had booked a room in town for them, and rented a movie, they ordered room service and settled in to watch the movie. As they sat on the bed he reached for her hand and kissed it, she was in heaven just sitting on the bed watching tv, 'god, I'm so low maintenance' she thought smiling to herself.

"What's so funny?" he said grabbing some popcorn from the bowl they were sharing.

"I was thinking how perfect this is," she said, "just you and me alone doing nothing but being together, it's funny."

He looked at her. "You are easily pleased." he said teasing her.

"I'm an easy sort of person I guess." she said. "I feel comfortable with you, this is nice."

"Yes." he agreed, "I think it will take some planning to get this time again, but we can enjoy it while we can." he said.

"I'm going to be in London by Saturday," she said, "then I have no idea when I'm going to be free to meet you, and you may not be free when I am." She frowned.

They snuggled up together and fell asleep. They were both exhausted. Suddenly Faith awoke and looked at the time:

"Oh my god I have to go," she said jumping off the bed, it was two a.m.

"Shit!" he said, "I'm so sorry Faith, I fell asleep."

"So did I!" she said. "I wish I could stay but, I don't have a phone at home and my mother will be frantic."

They grabbed their coats and left the comfort of the room, they started to walk to Faith's house, luckily it wasn't far. Faith's mother was still up waiting for Faith to get home, "Where the hell have you been, I've been worried sick!"

Tony jumped in, "I'm so sorry, we were watching a film and fell asleep. I'm sorry, it was my fault I've been working so much lately."

"No, it was my fault." Faith said, "I didn't sleep last night and was exhausted." Tony looked at her questioningly.

"Well okay," her mother said calmly.

"I assure you, Mrs Palmer, nothing has been going on, just we fell asleep, and I would never let anything happen to her." Tony said.

Her mother looked at the two of them and smiled, "Its okay, I think I know what's going on. You are making sure she doesn't see that boy again. Well she hasn't seen him, so you need not worry, and by Saturday she will be in London at that school for modelling away from him." Tony and Faith looked at each other.

"Okay now you're home I'm off to bed." her mother said yawning, "Goodnight Tony, nice to see you again."

He rushed an answer, "Yes nice to see you too, goodnight." When she had disappeared up the stairs, he looked into Faith's eyes and said "Why didn't you sleep last night?"

"Oh, just a bad dream." she said, as Tony grabbed Faith and gave her a passionate kiss.

"I wish you could have stayed with me tonight." he said.

She nodded, "I do too." She said, "but we have time to have that experience, I'm not going anywhere."

"Except Italy and America," he said laughing.

"Well I'm not going for two weeks, and I'll be in London which is not so far to come." she said.

"Yes, but we need to keep it very quiet Faith, no-one can know." he said.

"Well I'm not going to tell anyone, are you?" She said smiling.

"No, even though I want to shout it from the rafters." he said laughing. "I loved tonight," he said hugging her close.

"I did too," she said. "I'll call you when I get to my hotel on Saturday. I have no idea what time I will be there though." she said.

"That's okay, if I'm not at home the answering machine will be on." he said. "Can I see you in the morning before I go back to London or do you have to be somewhere?" he asked.

"What time do you have to check out?" She said.

"Eleven, but I'll catch the ten a.m. train back." he said.

"I'll be there at nine." She smiled.

"I'll look forward to it." he said. They kissed once more, and Tony started to walk back to the hotel. Suddenly he heard footsteps behind him.

He turned around to see Faith, "I left a note on the table telling my mum I had gone out early and won't be long." He looked at her, he couldn't believe she had done that to be with him. "She won't know," Faith said, "she was fast asleep when I went upstairs, she will think I went out in the morning, I just couldn't leave you all alone." she said smiling wickedly.

He looked serious for a moment. "Faith we can't do anything, you know that right?"

"I know." she said flippantly.

"I mean it, Faith, I can't risk any scandal."

Faith stopped and pulled him closer, "I know," she said, "I'm not going to have sex with you, I'm going to sleep with you, just to be close."

"Okay then." he said smiling as they got back to the hotel. Faith had grabbed a nightshirt from her room, and dressed in the bathroom. She sat on the bed as she watched Tony take his shirt off. "Hey turn around." he said smiling at Faith. She mockingly turned around as he got into the bed. They snuggled for a while and soon fell fast asleep, close to each other.

In the morning, she felt him still snuggled up to her, she turned around and kissed him; he responded, he kissed her neck. Down to her breasts, she took a deep breath. He couldn't stop once he had started and Faith never stopped him. Before they knew what they were doing, he was inside her, she gasped as they made love, he held her tightly as they moved in unison, kissing tenderly, as he came inside her, she moaned with pleasure as she pulsed around his firm manhood.

They held each other, he whispered in her ear, "I'm so sorry baby I couldn't fight it any longer, are you alright? I didn't hurt you, did I?"

"No," she said kissing him tenderly, "but we can't do this again, or you will get me pregnant, then we will be in trouble."

64

He moved away from her, "Oh god we didn't use anything."

She looked away. "Hopefully I'm not," she said "I've just come off, so it's probably okay." He hoped she was right.

Old Faith sat quietly watching her young self, with Tony, "Bloody hell!" she said, "I hope I'm not pregnant."

"You are not." the woman said.

"Phew." Faith took a deep breath.

"But your feelings for each other are growing deeper. I told you he wouldn't hurt you; I know this."

Faith looked unimpressed. "You don't know what I was like at that age," she said, "I couldn't get enough sex, and he looks like he can't cope without having her, me oh! You know."

"Yes, Faith I do know what you were like, I know everything about you, but you will cope and so will he." the woman replied...

Ted looked at Tony. "Where have you been? I've been trying to call you all night."

"I was out." Tony said slightly annoyed, "I am allowed a life you know!"

"Well," Ted said, "I can guess where you have been, and I'm really worried about you Tony. I know you, and you will not be able to keep your hands off her for long."

Tony looked a little embarrassed, Ted caught the look in Tony's eye. "Oh my god, you haven't?"

"No! no, I haven't." Tony lied, "but I see what you are saying, I can't help my feelings, it's so easy to forget how old she is, she doesn't act like she's fifteen at all."

"I'm not judging you, Tony, but the world will!" Ted said, looking worried for his friend.

That night Tony stayed at home. He couldn't go out with his friends, they would know there was something wrong. He wasn't his usual jolly self, full of pranks and fun, he didn't feel like having fun, he just wanted to crawl in a hole and die. He knew what Ted was saying, but he loved Faith with all his heart and didn't want to hurt her. He knew she would be in London for the next few weeks and if he could avoid seeing her at night, that would be a start.

But he needn't have worried so much, as the agency wouldn't let the girls out past nine p.m. and they kept them busy most of the day, so Faith only had mornings free, and Tony was in the studio until late. They grabbed breakfast together each day, then Faith spent an hour in the studio with Tony, before she had to go. She was so frustrated but she didn't want Tony to know how she felt or this might make things even worse. Every time she saw him, she ached for him. She had to hide it. Tony knew Faith was acting, pretending she didn't want him, and he had to hide his feelings too, it was for the best but it nearly killed him. The two weeks sped past and soon it was time for Faith to go to Italy.

Tony went to the airport with her carrying her luggage. He went to the gate and hugged her goodbye as he knew people were watching him.

"Keep in touch." he whispered to her.

"I will." she whispered back. As she disappeared through the gate he stood and watched the plane move away from the building, he stayed for a while wishing he had gone with her, but that wasn't possible and then people would know the truth, that he was in love with a minor.

# Chapter Six
## Separation

Faith was wrong about her timescale. She was in Italy for two months, working with the most amazing people. She was photographed with fabulous outfits and got to meet all the designers — she went to a lot of parties. Sophie was right, there were a lot of drugs but she turned them down and only drank water at the parties. She watched the other girls get drunk and high and didn't want any part of that, which caused some of the girls to think Faith thought she was better than them and made fun of her. At night she phoned Tony for an hour and then slept. She missed him terribly. However, she also knew as long as she spoke to him, he was still hers.

Still, Tony was miserable, he kept it together when he was working but felt the emptiness when he went home, so he pushed for a longer time in the studio, working alone a lot of the time. He made sure his phone call with Faith happened, then went straight back to work. Ted's wedding came up, and Faith was working and couldn't get away. Tony was very upset, he was looking forward to her being there with him, but there was nothing she could do, she was locked into a contract. Tony knew how this felt, as his band had been locked into contracts before and had got ripped off.

Ted was happy with his life and knew that Faith had saved him from certain death, he struggled for a while with the decision but decided that this was his life now. Even though Kate thought he couldn't have changed his mind that quickly she went along with it, as she loved Ted dearly.

He had been so much more attentive, "I don't know what happened," she said to Pete's wife Amanda, "but I'm glad it did."

"Yes, I'm sure you are relieved, you both look so happy."

"We are." Ted said as he came up behind his new wife.

It was a lovely day, the sun shone all day, all their friends and family attended the wedding. Everyone noticed how shut off Tony seemed, but were under strict instructions not to broach the subject with him; Ted had his back as usual.

The months went by, Faith finally left Italy and the other girls that were constantly horrible to her. She went to America and did the commercial with John Wayne. He invited her to his ranch for a month, but a month turned into two. She was enjoying the time spent riding and learning to drive a car, she started to race in bangers and went on to bigger races. She got very good at it — she enjoyed the rush of going fast. The lovely conversations with John and talking about her aspirations and her views on life and such. She attended a lot of Hollywood parties and met some of the people she had only seen in movies, it was thrilling. The time difference made it hard to keep up the phone calls, and by the time she came home to England, Tony was on tour again.

She managed to get Ted on the phone once, and he told her how miserable Tony was especially now that she was dating John Wayne's son,

"WHAT! I'm not dating anyone but Tony!"

"That's not what we heard." Ted said.

"Can you get him to call me, please Ted." she pleaded, but as she was giving him the number Ted misheard the number and Tony couldn't get through. He tried everything, he called her agency but they wouldn't give him the number of where she was.

"I'm her boyfriend." he hissed.

"I don't care who you are," the receptionist said, "it's against our policy to give out numbers, even if you say you are her boyfriend." So he left a message for her to call him, but the receptionist didn't like Faith, so the message wasn't passed on.

Faith was panic-stricken, she couldn't let Tony think she was with someone else, she would never cheat on him. The newspaper dropped on the doormat, she read it while she was eating breakfast, she went straight to the entertainment section. They were in the news, there was a picture of the band and kissing Tony was a beautiful brunette. Tony didn't look like he was shocked, she scrunched the paper up and threw it on the floor and went back to bed and cried herself to sleep.

A few weeks later Faith had been offered a job in Saudi Arabia, with twenty other girls. It was a job of a lifetime, and the pay was more money than she had ever been offered before, she would be a fool not to take it.

They would have pictures with a Saudi prince, they had to dress like wives of the prince in beautiful long dresses, embellished with gold, and pretend they were at a function with the royal family. They had to cover their heads with silk scarves, they had the most beautiful jewellery on, lots of gold and gem stones.

The prince's uncle noticed Faith's stunning eyes. He remembered a woman he was in love with, a married woman, who had the same eyes. She lived in India, the wife of the district commissioner, her husband was away on business, and she was a guest of the Rajah at his palace. Of course, she didn't give him the time of day, she was busy with her two small children and liked the company of the Russian diplomats who were also guests of the Rajah, but he never forgot her.

Faith had told him her grandparents lived in India. They moved to England in 1935, her grandfather was a circuit judge in India, when they went to England he took the bar. They chatted for a long time about her family and how they came to England, and soon he realised that the woman he had loved, was her grandmother. He was very happy that she had a perfect life, and Faith was just like her.

The prince had noticed her too and spoke to her about his family and his pure bred race horses, he promised to show her the next day. He couldn't take his eyes off her, as they stood with glasses of champagne. He was very close to her, he could smell her perfume. She noticed he was standing very close and stepped away from him, all the other girls noticed, most of them looked on in good humour, but a couple of the girls were very jealous and tried to get some attention from the prince. The prince was not impressed with their behaviour and sent them away, he didn't like pushy women, Faith was easy to talk to, and it soon became apparent he was falling in love with her and asked her to be his wife. Faith had to turn him down saying her heart belonged to another, she hoped this was true as she hadn't spoken to Tony in months. Christmas had gone by, and he had forgotten her sixteenth birthday and not a word from him. She had stopped calling him as she felt everyone would have thought she was desperate. The prince wasn't pleased with her refusal, but wished her well.

Faith could only think about Tony, he was all she wanted in her life. The prince was very friendly and very good looking, but she didn't have any feelings towards him, apart from he was a nice man. He enjoyed her company, his uncle clapped him on the back laughing, "never mind my prince, I know how you feel, I also was dismissed by her grandmother many years ago."

The job ended, and Faith accompanied by the other girls returned to England. Faith had decided to use the money to buy a flat in London but found she could only have a bedsit as she was too young to get a mortgage.

# Chapter Seven
## Reunited

The months went by and not a word from Tony; Faith felt destroyed. She went to work and went home, she didn't speak to anyone. She never went out with her new friends, they constantly asked her to go nightclubbing with them. Still, she didn't want to go, and every time she did give in and go out with them; she had creepy men asking her out, she just couldn't be bothered.

She had moved into her small bedsit as she needed her own space. The months rolled by, and it was her seventeenth birthday. Her friends decided to take her racing at Brands Hatch. She only went because they told her, if she didn't, they would make her life a misery, she was already miserable, she couldn't imagine what they could do to her. Still, she indulged them, she just hoped she didn't bump into that annoying guy, who every time he saw her asked her out. She didn't find him in the least bit appealing plus he was quite nasty when she turned him down.

Once at the racecourse she did enjoy watching the cars race past and even got invited to race the teen race, her reputation for racing had preceded her. She put on the team overalls and crash helmet and got into the car she was racing. The race began, she kept very good time, she didn't win, but she did have fun. As she got out of the car she bumped into that annoying guy (she never caught his name), he grinned at her, but she made out she hadn't seen him. He was with a couple of other men,

"There she is, the fridge, I bet she's gay." she overheard him say. He was talking to one of the men with him, as he turned around, they both laughed, the other man didn't turn around but told him to be quiet as she might hear him. She didn't see his face but heard his voice it was unmistakable, he had cut his hair, but she knew who it was. She started to shake first with anger then she couldn't hold back the tears, she still had her crash hat on so they couldn't see her face, she brushed past them, as one of her friends called her name,

"Hurry up Faith, they are getting drinks in."

Suddenly she felt someone grab her hand, "Faith?" his voice said. She pulled away angrily, then she saw his beautiful face.

"Leave me alone." she said as forcefully as she could, but he didn't let go. He pushed up her visor the tears streamed down her face, she could hardly see,

"Oh, Faith I've been looking everywhere for you."

"Don't lie to me Tony and let me go."

She took off her helmet and threw it at him. He caught it and placed it on the floor. "Please Faith let me explain." he said.

She narrowed her eyes, "Oh go on then, I would love to hear it!"

He held her close to him, trying to hug her. Still, she struggled, one of the men she was with, in the racing team, asked if there was a problem as Faith was getting loud, "NO!" they both replied. He backed away, Tony couldn't hide his amusement.

"Oh, fuck no," a voice from behind him, the guy she had turned down so royally was standing behind Tony, "you know her?"

"Yes." Tony said. "I'm sorry guys I need to go, see you another time."

"what the fuck!" Tony's friend said. "I don't believe this."

The other man said "I guess she's not gay, just not into you," laughing.

"What has he got that I don't?" said his friend.

His other friend was laughing so much he almost fell over saying "He has everything." He shrugged his shoulders and went back to where they were standing, watching with disdain as Tony and Faith walked away.

Faith was a mess. "Please Tony, let me go, I can't do this." she blubbered.

"No, I won't, I need to know what happened," he said trying to keep her from running, "who's this guy you are seeing? Where is he?" He sounded angry now.

"What? I'm not seeing anyone, what are you talking about?"

"I saw a picture of you in a magazine, you were with John Wayne, and you were standing next to his son, and it said you were seeing him." Tony said.

"He's bloody fourteen, you idiot! Why on earth would I be dating him?" she said in disbelief.

"Then when you stopped calling me, I thought it was true." he said looking miserable.

"Well you shouldn't believe everything you read Tony, you told me that," she snapped, "and I stopped calling because you were never there when I called. I fell asleep before you woke up. It was getting ridiculous. And what about that woman you're seeing, the one with brown hair, she was kissing you!"

Faith's friends came back to see where she had got to, "Faith, are you coming?"

"No, she isn't." Tony snapped.

"Oh okay!" Her friend snapped back.

"Actually yes, I am." Faith said following her friend.

Tony trailed behind. "Now where are you going?" he asked.

"I'm going to get fucking drunk if you want to know" she said defiantly.

"Oh no you're not!" he said grabbing her hand again.

"Is this the guy?" her friend said.

"Yes" Faith said shakily.

"Well don't you think you need to talk to him then?" Her friend said.

"Why, and let him make even more of a fool of me." she retorted.

"Faith I never meant to make a fool out of you," Tony said almost whispering, "please talk to me."

Faith couldn't look at him. "I can't, please go away." she said as she started to cry again. He grabbed her around her waist and drew her into him and she melted into a pool of misery, "I missed you so much Tony." she mumbled.

"I missed you too baby, please, let's go back to my flat and talk about it, I'm so sorry." His voice was quivering as she could hear the emotion in his throat. Her friend gave her the handbag she was holding for her, and Faith left with Tony.

As she sat in his car, she looked at his face, it was very red and his neck was blotchy. He didn't say a word while he was driving the forty-five minutes to his flat, it was agony, as he pulled into his parking space and turned off the engine, he got out of the car and opened her door. She took his hand and stepped out of the car, she was still crying, he led her to his front door and fumbled for his keys. "Fuck" he said in frustration, as he finally opened the door, he turned on the lights, he couldn't contain himself any longer, a single tear rolled down his face, "I didn't leave you Faith, you have to believe me."

"I didn't leave you either," she said angrily, "I loved you and you left me." she shouted.

"No, I didn't, I swear to god, I didn't."

"Well I don't believe in bloody god, so don't swear to him." she said.

He looked shocked. "Really?" he said.

"What?"

"You don't believe in god."

"No, why, what's that got to do with anything?" she said.

"Oh nothing," he said, "but Faith you have to believe me." She sat on his sofa and grabbed some tissues from her bag.

"So why didn't you call me?" she said.

"I didn't have your number! Either Ted wrote it down wrong, or you said it wrong, I don't know, I tried to call you, but the number was wrong," he said.

"This was supposed to be the happiest time of my life." she said blowing her nose.

"What?" he asked.

"It's my birthday." she replied.

"Is it? Oh no." he moaned, "And I forgot."

"Yes, you forgot me last year too. Everyone forgot, even my mother didn't send me a card." she said blowing her nose again.

"Do you remember what I said to you about your birthday?" He said.

"Yes, you said you won't take me home."

"Yes, and I meant it," he said.

"But you forgot all about me." she said looking him in the eyes.

He looked down. "I'm so sorry, time goes so fast when you are on tour, and we have been on tour almost solidly. I meant what I said though I don't want to take you home."

"Well I can't hold you to it, now can I?" she said starting to cry all over again. He sat on the sofa next to her, he felt miserable too, he put his arms around her and pulled her to him.

"I thought I would never see you again," he said, "but here you are, my Faith."

"I'm not your Faith anymore," she said, through her tears, "you don't know me anymore, I'm not that little girl you met two years ago." she said with the tears rolling down her cheeks.

"You smell the same," he said, then he looked into her face "same eyes, a bit wet, but the same." He was trying to make her smile, but she had been putting a brave face on for so long she couldn't manage even the slightest smile. She was unbelievably sad. "Have I lost you?" he said.

"I don't know. Have I lost you?" she replied.

"I will always love you Faith, I never stopped, this has been the hardest thing I've ever done, I've never waited two years for someone." he said.

"Actually, if you count the married sex it's been eighteen months." she said.

"The what?" he said laughing, "married sex?"

"Yes, it wasn't passionate, it was comforting, that's married sex," she said. "I've dreamt of that night so many times. At first it kept me happy, but then I started to have bad dreams about the time I saw the picture of you with that woman." she said, trembling.

"Faith I was posing that's all, it wasn't anything, I promise you." he said. He was telling the truth, he didn't even know the woman's name. "And I had to go to Ted's wedding without you," he said, "I hated every moment you were away, trying to keep up with where you were was a nightmare, and I even phoned Sophie. Of course, she told me to fuck off", he said.

"Why? Why would she do that?" Faith asked.

"Oh, that's another story, I used to date her," he said, "then I didn't. I just dumped her and she thought I had done the same to you. So basically, she told me to leave you alone to get over me, like she had to," he said, "but Faith I don't want you to get over me. Can we please start again? This time we don't have to hide from anyone. Maybe people will say stuff, they always do, but it won't be illegal," he said, "we could get married, that's what we talked about."

Faith looked at Tony. "Do you mean it Tony, you want to get married?"

"I want you, and only you, so yes, marriage, we could go to Las Vegas; it takes two days to get married there."

"Is that legal?" Faith said, wiping her eyes.

"Yes, I think so, I know loads of people who have done that, are you still working?"

"My contract just finished so I was going to leave it a couple of months then go to the States to work; I've had loads of offers of work there," she said.

"I don't want you working away any more, it's too hard to keep phoning, plus I'm sure you can work with me, we are doing videos with our music now"

"Yes, I've seen them, not my thing, Tony." she said, "but I can work in London, that way I'll be home at night," she said.

"Home," he said "that has a nice ring to it, but I want you with me when I'm touring, how do you feel about that?" he said. "I'm sure any agency could work around that."

"I don't know, I must earn money," she said.

"Why? If we are married my money will be yours." he said.

"I'm not good at not paying my way Tony, I need some independence." she said.

"Can we work the details out tomorrow?" He said, "I'm tired and hungry, and I'm sure you are too."

"I could eat something." she replied.

Tony started to get the takeaway menus from his kitchen "What do you fancy? Chinese, Indian?"

"I guess Chinese," she said, "I usually cook myself, that way I know what's in it," she said

"Okay, Chinese it is." He picked up the phone, she pointed out the things she wanted, and he ordered it. The food arrived thirty minutes later.

"That was quick," she said getting the plates out of Tony's kitchen.

"Yes, the takeaway is just around the corner," he said watching her opening drawers to find forks. She set them on the table, and they sat down to eat. Faith had calmed down a lot now and was thinking about the conversation they were having, Tony put the food on the plates.

"So what kind of food do you eat now then," he said, "lettuce?" he laughed.

"I eat good food," she said "only real meat and lots of fresh vegetables. I make things from scratch you know? I guess that's old fashioned, but I like to know what I'm putting into my body. It has to be balanced, not too much of anything like pastry, but if I do eat things like that, I make it myself. Dumplings and cakes are okay, but again I have to make them myself. I had to learn to cook as my mother stopped for some reason, I guess she wanted us to be more independent, so I learned to cook the things I like, of course.

"If you cook and most of the other girls don't, they tend to come over for girly nights more at my place than theirs. It's always good to share, then you don't eat too much. Or I'll freeze it in portions as I'm away a lot and don't always have time to go shopping or cook from scratch." she said.

"Sounds like a lot of work to me." he said.

"No not really, I like cooking, it keeps me busy. I have needed to be busy, or I just crash out and don't open my door to anyone, or answer my phone." she said sadly.

"That's all over now Faith, I promise you." he said, "I will never leave your side again."

"That could be difficult for you, people will think I've got you on a leash, and I don't want people to think that way about me."

"Who cares what people think, the people who care about us will know the truth. So where are you living now," he said, "are you back at home with your mother?"

"No, I moved out a few months ago, I bought a bedsit. It's small, but I don't need much room, as I'm not there much." she said

"Faith," he said suddenly, "I don't want to take you home, move in here with me," he said.

"I don't know, I need to think about that Tony, it's not a small thing you are asking." She looked down at the floor, "I'm afraid." she said.

Old Faith knew that feeling well. She wanted her young self to be happy, she knew the signs that her younger self was actually in love with this man. He seemed to be equally in love with her, it was strange to see both sides as an outsider, she knew it was herself but, felt like it was her child. She had been married at sixteen and had her first child at sixteen also, so she knew she was mature enough for marriage and children as she had already done it. Unfortunately, her husband wasn't mature enough, and so it ended. Tony was a full-grown man; he had experienced life at its worse and its best; he must know what he wants. Faith started to trust that he was telling the truth.

Ted knocked on the door, no answer, the lights were on, but it seemed Tony wasn't in. He knocked again, he shouted through the letterbox "Come on Tony let me in." Tony opened the door looking sheepish. "Oh my god you have a bird in there, don't you? I know that look, finally, I thought you were broken." he laughed.

"I'm not broken any more," he said, "but I need some privacy Ted, is it important?"

"Well, not anything that can't wait 'till tomorrow but then everyone will know, and I wanted to tell you first."

"Okay, come in, but not a word, okay?" Tony said.

"Okay," Ted said as he went into the living room, "Faith! Wow! I never thought I would see you again." He looked at her and noticed the blotchy face and knew she had been crying.

He looked at Tony quizzically, Tony shrugged his shoulders looking very guilty, Faith got up and gave Ted a hug.

"Hello Ted, how are you? I'm sorry I couldn't make your wedding," she said

"Oh yes, talking about weddings Ted," said Tony "can you get time free to fly to Vegas next week, we are getting married."

Ted's face was a mixture of confusion and happiness, "You two? Next week!" he said in disbelief.

"Yes," Tony said.

Faith looked a little embarrassed "I know it's sudden." she said.

"No, no it isn't sudden. You have waited two years for this Tony, I know how you have suffered, now it will be all right and you will both be happy." He smiled at them both, then laughed, "and you can stop writing shit songs about lost loves." he laughed again nudging Tony. Tony looked embarrassed now, "I'm so happy for you both and guess what, Kate and I are having a baby!" Ted announced

"What? That's amazing." Tony said. "I thought you were never going to have one, how many years have you been together?"

"Seven years," Ted said laughing "but we were too poor to have a child before.".

They talked for a little while then Ted went home.

Tony looked at Faith. "Alone at last." he said menacingly. Faith looked genuinely scared. Tony wrapped his arms around her, "Don't worry Faith we don't have to have married sex if you don't want."

They both laughed. "I'm not prepared Tony, I don't even have spare underwear." she said.

"That's okay you can use mine," he joked, "you can have anything out of my wardrobe, I'm sure there will be something you can wear. I think I have a spare toothbrush as I pinch them from the hotels we stay at."

Faith relaxed a little. "Do you have any booze?"

"I don't think that's a good idea Faith," he said.

"It's all right, I'm not thinking of getting drunk now Tony," she said.

"Okay I have some vodka." he said.

"Anything else?" she said pulling a face.

"Let's go and have a look. I've been away, so I've forgotten what is there… nothing." he said as he looked in the empty cupboard, "I can go to the off-licence if you want?"

"Can I use your shower?" she said.

"Of course. All the nicked stuff is in the drawer under the sink, it's better than men's aftershave." he laughed, "What do you want to drink?" he asked

"Can you get a white wine, a sweet one something like a Blue Nun?"

"Ok I won't be long." He left her looking at all the shampoos and body washes he had pilfered from various hotels they had stayed at. Some of it was actually really nice.

As she was relaxing in the hot shower, Tony came back with the wine, "Sorry I was so long," he said, "the queue was horrendous."

He put the wine in the fridge and entered the bathroom, "Mind if I join you?" he said softly. She opened the door for him, he took off his clothes and joined her in the hot shower. She soaped him all over his chest and down his front, he took a deep breath, he kissed her passionately and pushed her against the wall kissing and caressing her breasts. She gasped with delight, the soap ran down her body as he kissed her more and more passionately, he turned her around and held her tightly as he entered her from behind. She was so wet he slipped inside easily, she moaned as he thrust inside her.

He hadn't had sex since the last time with Faith so it didn't take long for him to climax, but he didn't stop until she begged him, "harder", she said as he thrust harder. He was in agony but kept on until she screamed with delight. He held himself inside her until the pain had subsided. They held on to each other for a little while, she turned around and kissed him tenderly, she washed his back as he shampooed his hair, they finished the shower and got out.

Wrapped in towels they went to the bedroom, he sat on the side of the bed looking at his prize lovingly. She straddled his lap kissing his neck and face, then he flicked her nipples with his tongue. She pushed him down and his sizable erection slid easily inside her once more. She rode him gently as he massaged her breasts, she reached another climax just as he did, they clung to each other until the feeling subsided and fell onto the bed.

He wrapped his arms around her rolling over so she was on her back, she laughed as she tried to put him back on to his back but this time, he didn't allow her to, she realised how strong he was, this pleased her. He looked at her "I really missed you Faith." he said in earnest

"I missed you too." she said teary-eyed.

"Please don't cry any more, baby. I promise you I will never leave you to fend for yourself again."

"I understand why we couldn't be together before" she said.

"It still wasn't fun though was it." he said.

"No but if we hadn't, you would have got into so much trouble." she said.

"Yes, it could have seriously damaged my career, and the bands. But let's not dwell on it any more we have reached the goal post, and I'm never letting you go again." he said smiling.

Tony got up and got the wine and two glasses. While she was pouring the wine, he went to the bathroom to wash her off him. When he returned, he lay on the bed as she passed him his glass, then she tipped some of the wine over him and sucked it off, he gasped as she licked and sucked his manhood. They kissed and petted for hours, the wine drunk and them exhausted, they fell asleep holding tightly onto each other.

# Chapter Eight
## The Ring

The next morning, they showered and dressed. Faith was wearing Tony's shirt and his underpants, but had her jeans on as his were too big and looked a little silly. She loved the shirt it was silky and a bit flash, she liked his style. She tousled his wet hair with her fingers, "Next time you have your hair cut," she said, "can you save some for me?"

"What my hair?" he said puzzled.

"Yes, I don't want the coloured bit, it has to be natural."

"What do you want that for?" he said.

"I just do," she said, "I'll show you when you give it to me." He thought nothing of it. "I need to go to my flat and get some clothes," she said "that is if you want me to stay over again?"

"I don't want you to stay over Faith," he said, as he held her close to him, "I want you to move in here with me."

"Are you sure Tony?" she said with a worried look on her face.

"I'm sure." Tony said, kissing her lips tenderly, she nodded and kissed him back.

After they had some tea and toast, Tony drove to Faith's flat. It wasn't very far, and Faith was right, it was very small. Still, it was very tasteful and tidy. He sat on her huge sofa while she got a bag together, "This is nice" he said as he watched her pack.

"Yes, it was a dump when I bought it but a little tender loving care and now it's not that bad. It looks smaller than it is, I just had to have that sofa, you can just get lost in it, and it's ever so comfortable too." she said. "I have no idea how we are going to get it out of here, you should have seen the delivery men trying to get it in. I've even got a little balcony." He looked out the door to see a small balcony with pots filled with tomato plants and cucumber plants and some herbs, a small table and two chairs

"That's sweet," he said, "how will you feel letting this go?"

"Well I won't sell it, I'll just rent it out," she said.

"Why? Do you think you would need it?" He said looking worried.

"No, I just think it would be a good investment." she said, "Tony if we get married, I would never leave you, plus what would we do with our thousands of children in a place this small." she smiled.

"Is that a smile?" he said, "So having children will make you happy?"

"I told you when we met, I wanted a family. I don't care how many children we have, do you?"

"Not really," he said, "but I don't think we should start a family until we get a bigger house, my flat is okay for us but not kids, I want a garden you know, space to run about." he said.

"Yes, I agree," she said, as she closed her bag, "all done. I can come back later for the rest," she said.

She looked at him and smiled and said "If we carry on like last night, Tony I'll be pregnant before the end of the week." she laughed.

"It was heaven last night, Faith, I do realise it won't be like that all the time," he said, "but for the first time in ages all that pent-up frustration just disappeared."

"Yes, I enjoyed it too." She said, "I'm still scared but…"

"What are you scared of Faith? Dragons and ogres, I'll fight them, they won't get you." he laughed.

"I'm frightened of this not being what I think it is, and we are making a terrible mistake, why do you want me?"

He took her hand tenderly, "Faith listen to me, I have loved you from the first moment I saw you in your mother's house two years ago today actually. You are beautiful, funny, clever, you obviously are older than your years, I don't know another seventeen year old who can provide themselves, not only with a job that pays well, and a flat of their own," he said looking around, "and you have style."

"You helped me with the job remember, then everything fell into my lap." she argued.

"Even if I did help you in the beginning you managed to keep the job for nearly two years," he said, "you are more beautiful than you were then, if that's possible, even when you are angry and sobbing you are more beautiful than anyone I know. We will be happy I know it, and if we are not all these months of misery was for nothing." he said. "I'm going to tell you something only Ted knows, I was so unhappy I was thinking of giving up the band and going back home and living like a hermit."

"Liar!" she said pushing him, he stumbled into his car laughing.

"I'm not lying, Faith, I was on the verge of suicide." he said.

"Don't ever say that again!" she snapped. "Your life was a gift, you have to live it before you give it back."

"I have lived." he said. "I've had experiences a lot of people haven't had, but without you Faith what's the point?"

"I'm here Tony, I'm not going anywhere unless you tell me you don't want me, I promise I won't leave."

He looked at her, "This life isn't for everyone Faith, but if it comes to the job or you, I would choose you."

"Well luckily for you I would never make you choose," she said.

"Look now I have to make up for forgetting your birthday, what do you want Faith? Anything." She looked at him and waved her hand. He knew exactly what she wanted. "Okay then let's go ring shopping." He was beaming.

"Well that was easy," she said, doing her seatbelt up. He drove into town and parked behind the shops. "You can't park here Tony it's private."

"That's okay darling I know the owners, I can't just walk up the high street you know." He opened her door and held his hand out for her to get out. As they walked through the back door of a shop he shouted, "Oi. Anyone home?"

A man got up from an easy chair, putting down his cup of tea, "Tony, you old bugger, where have you been?"

"Oh about, you know me. I'm looking for something special today," Tony said.

The man looked at Faith. "Of course you are. Necklace? Bracelet?"

"No, engagement ring," he said, looking at Faith lovingly.

"Bloody hell boy, she put an end to your shenanigans, has she?" he laughed.

Tony looked at the man shaking his head and frowning "What are you like?" he said "just get me something to look at will you?"

"Oh yes, sorry." The man said and hurriedly opened a case at the back wall of the shop.

Tony looked at Faith, "Matty here knows everything there is to know about fine jewellery, I'm sure there will be something you will like Faith." There were three trays of really expensive looking rings on the counter, Faith looked at them closely. She picked one up, it was massive on her slim finger, the man took her hand and slipped a ring gauge on her ring finger.

"Okay those are way too big." He put the trays away and replaced them with some others. Faith gravitated to the silver looking ones, of course they were platinum. She picked another one up and tried it on.

"How much is this?" she asked.

"Never you mind how much they are Faith, just have the one you like." Tony said. She looked at the tray where she saw the price was inside the groove, she put the ring back quickly. Tony laughed, "I said it doesn't matter how much it costs if you like it, that's the one you will have."

"Oh no I couldn't." she said in horror, Tony laughed. Matty put another tray in front of Faith.

"These are the best diamonds you will find in London, love." Faith saw the one. She always seemed to know instantly she saw things if it was right or not. It was so pretty. She looked at Tony wide-eyed.

"You like that one?" he said.

"Is it expensive?" she said looking worried.

"Nothing is too expensive for you." Tony said honestly, "you can have it if that's the one, okay. Matty check the sizing mate and we will have that one." Matty looked very pleased. Faith was very uncomfortable, she had never had someone spend money on her like this, the ring fitted perfectly.

"Are you wearing it now or do you want it in the box?" Matty said smiling. Faith didn't want to take it off it was so shiny it glistened on her finger.

"She will wear it," Tony said, "but I'll have the box so she has somewhere to put it when she wants to hide it from her mother." They all laughed but Faith thought her mother would have a fit if she knew she was getting married, and didn't tell her. Tony settled up with Matty, and Faith and Tony left the shop.

"Can I get married without my mother's permission?" Faith said on the way back to the flat.

"I don't think so, that's why we need to go and see her."

"What! I haven't seen her in months; she will be spiteful, I know it." she said.

"No, she won't, I'll be with you, and if she does, we will just have to wait to get married. Anyway, she didn't seem that bothered you were going to marry that Martin guy, so why would she be bothered if you marry me?" Tony said.

"I don't know, she has this habit of doing the exact opposite of what you expect, so your guess is as good as mine." Faith said.

"Well we need to go to find out, we will go tomorrow okay?" he said.

"Okay but I won't be responsible for the things she says okay?" she said.

"Okay." Tony laughed.

The next day they drove to Faith's mother's house, and parked outside. Faith panicked.

"I can't Tony what if she says no?"

"I told you, it's not a problem we can wait, but we have to try. Okay, are you ready?" he said they got out of the car.

Faith knocked on the door, her mother answered, "Oh look at you, Miss Fancy Pants," she said smiling "how are you dear?" Faith looked at Tony and shrugged her shoulders as they walked into the house, "… and Tony so nice to see you too. How's the job going Faith?" her mother said going into the kitchen.

"I'm on a break right now mum, my contract finished. We are deciding what to take next as I don't want to leave England right now."

"Oh? Why's that I thought you love travelling, tea?" Her mother said.

"Yes, please, I do, but I miss Tony, so …"

"Tony?" Her mother said, "Oh, I see, are you seeing him now?"

"Well Mrs Palmer, we are getting married and wondered if you would give your permission so we can marry next week," Tony explained.

"How long have you been seeing Faith?" she asked.

"Not long, but now we've decided to marry and need your permission."

"Yes, you said that," she said, "well I always did like you Tony, so have you got the paperwork for me to sign?"

"Yes, I do," he said, as he pulled out a piece of paper from his jacket. Faith was stunned. Her mother looked over the piece of paper Tony gave her.

"Okay then, that's done," she said as she signed it. Tony put the signed papers back into the pocket of his jacket.

"Where did you get that?" Faith asked.

"I got it over a year ago," Tony said, "I'm sorry I should have told you, but things got in the way, and I forgot until last night that I even had it, but it makes things so much easier doesn't it"? He said.

"Yes, it does." Faith said as her mother grabbed her hand and looked at the ring that Tony had bought her.

"Oh, my what a lovely ring," she said "that must have cost a lot of money Tony."

"Nothing is too much for Faith." Tony smiled lovingly, "Anyway, would you like to come to the wedding? It's going to be in America."

"Oh, I can't fly dear, I'm afraid I can't, but you take lots of pictures, won't you? I'm sure you will be fine without me there, won't you Faith?" her mother said.

"Yes, but wouldn't you like to be there, Mum?" Faith said.

"It's an aeroplane Faith, I tried to get on one to go to Jersey, you remember I just couldn't do it.". her mother said.

"Oh yes, I forgot, sorry. We will send you pictures." Faith said.

"That would be lovely." her mother said. As they were leaving Faith's mother gave Faith a hug "I do love you Faith, don't forget that." she said as she let go.

Faith looked at her mother, she felt very confused. "I love you too Mum. Take care. See you soon." she said.

"Well you know where I am." She said as they left the house. Tony opened the car door for Faith to get in. "Take care of yourself, won't you dear." her mother said.

"Yes. Bye." Faith said wondering what had just happened. This was a first.

The drive back was tense.

"What's wrong Faith?" Tony said.

"I don't know." she said. "She's never been bothered about me, why was she so nice?"

"Maybe she missed you, I know I did when I hadn't seen you in months."

"Maybe." Faith agreed.

"I got that marriage paperwork after you left for Italy. I had every intention of telling you, but it was so hard to talk over the phone, and I wanted to tell you to your face. I only remembered it this morning as I was trying to think how would we get permission" he said.

"Lucky you did. I was wondering how we were going to get it too. But there it is in black and white," Faith said.

"I don't know if we need it in America, but we have it, if we do." he said. Faith relaxed and smiled as she thought about her wedding.

"What's next?" she said.

"I think a wedding dress." said Tony.

"Are you wearing a tuxedo?" Faith asked.

"Maybe," he said coyly.

"Oh, it's like that, is it?" she laughed. He nodded. "Can I invite John?"

"What John Wayne?" he said.

"Yes."

"Do you think he will come?" he said.

"I don't know, it depends on where it is and what he's doing at the time, I guess. Mind you he might not, as I don't want a religious ceremony."

Tony looked at Faith. "You don't want all the church and flowers and stuff?"

"I would like the flowers but not a priest." she said, "I did tell you I don't believe in God, didn't I?"

"Yes, but I thought you were angry and just said it." He said.

"A celebrant is fine," she said looking at Tony, "unless you want the church and everything."

"I don't believe in god either. I just don't tell people that as they want to know why and then there's a big debate, and I don't really like getting into the whys and wherefores." Tony said.

Faith nodded. "It's not my favourite subject either," she said.

It was late when they got back to London.

"Are you hungry?" he said.

"Yes, but it's too late to cook anything." she said.

He pulled over in front of a fancy looking restaurant. "Let's see if we can get a table here. Stay in the car, and I'll go and see."

Tony got out of the car and disappeared into the restaurant. He seemed to be gone for a long time, then he came back to the car. He opened the door for Faith to get out. "They can fit us in." he said smiling. They got shown to a small table for two. The restaurant was cosy and quiet, with clean white table cloths and a single candle in the centre of the table. The waiting staff bustled about serving the customers. Faith noticed how quiet it was in the restaurant as they ordered their food and Tony ordered the wine. The food was delicious and in no time, Faith was full and happy, as they finished and Tony paid the bill, he said "let's go home."

As they arrived back at Tony's flat Ted turned up with all their friends and dragged them to a club. He had booked a private party and made sure they were the only people in the club as quite a few of their friends were famous. Faith was star struck most of the evening, if it wasn't for Kate, Pamela and Amanda she didn't think she would have got through it. Unfortunately, Faith had too much to drink too quickly and landed up being sick in the loos for half the evening. Tony had to take her home and put her to bed.

She felt so ashamed. "I'm so sorry Tony." she kept on saying as she was lying in bed. Tony was not angry at all, had seen his friends plying her with booze and someone had definitely spiked her drinks. He would be having words with his friends when he saw them next.

The next day Faith was up early making bacon and eggs for breakfast.

"What no hangover?" Tony said quite shocked.

"No, I don't suffer from those," she said, "but I don't usually get that drunk, I'm so sorry Tony you must think I'm a lightweight, did I embarrass you? That's why I stick to wine." she said.

"I wasn't embarrassed," he said, "I was worried though, you looked so ill."

"I felt ill! What was in those drinks?"

"I have no idea." he said, "but I'm not happy with the person who gave them to you."

She looked at Tony. "Don't look at me. I don't know who he was." she said, "They are your friends."

# Chapter Nine
## The wedding

They spent the next week getting ready to go to Las Vegas; Faith had bought a beautiful dress and some jewels to go in her hair, she wasn't going to wear shoes. Ted liked that, he commented on being barefoot and pregnant. Faith wasn't bothered, she didn't know about how they both came into her life and turned it into a fairy tale, they would never tell her either, it was their secret. But she loved them both dearly and couldn't imagine living without them now. Tony took such great care of her; he was like the proverbial knight in shining armour, the sex wasn't bad either.

Old Faith was loving watching the preparations of her wedding and loved the styles that Faith chose. 'Of course, I would love it' she thought, 'it's my taste. I never had the money or the freedom to choose what I wanted before.' She liked that Tony allowed Faith all the freedom she wanted, but noticed Faith was very frugal, she never seemed to waste money.

Ted and Kate travelled with Tony and Faith to Las Vegas, Kate was only a few months pregnant, so travelling wasn't difficult for her. Still, Ted was very protective of her, asking if she was comfortable and if she needed anything every five minutes, it was lovely to see Ted acting like a mother hen, Tony laughed, Faith smiled hoping Tony would be the same when she was in that position.

They had booked into a very nice hotel. Their rooms were next to each other which probably wasn't the best idea as Tony and Faith were very noisy during the night, and Kate needed more sleep than usual. By the morning Kate wasn't in the best of moods, of course. Ted tried to console her with ordering her the biggest breakfast he could. It worked, as she ate her food enjoying every bite. Tony and Faith arrived and ordered some eggs and coffee.

Faith was very red as she was aware that Ted and Kate would have heard them the night before, Faith was a very shy person in reality and wasn't used to other people knowing what she was doing with her lover. Ted made fun of her and told her not to worry what other people think so much, as he understood how they felt, he didn't think he would have coped so well waiting to be with the one he loved, above all others, Faith appreciated his honesty but still apologised to Kate for keeping her awake and promised to try to be quiet the next night, Tony just smiled.

Kate and Faith went to the beauty parlour to get their hair and nails done; Faith had made sure the beautician could do her toenails as she wanted glittery varnish with tiny diamonds set in them, and matching her hands, they looked very shiny. Then returned to their rooms to put their makeup on and dress for the wedding.

Ted and Tony spent the time gambling in the casino, they both came out a lot better off, and in plenty of time to have a shower. Tony took his chips to the cash desk and cashed them in. Ted tossed his chips on top of Tony's and said "You can have mine too, call it a wedding present." Laughing. Tony took the money and went back to the room.

By this time the girls were ready and waiting in Ted and Kate's room. Ted went into the bathroom smiling at his wife, she looked stunning. After he had his shower and got dressed, they went downstairs together to the chapel and waited for Tony.

The ceremony was short and sweet, and there were quite a lot of pictures taken by the photographer they had hired to cover the wedding. It was how Faith wanted it, all she cared about was that she was married to the love of her life, and he loved her, unconditionally. John had sent a wonderful gift and an apology as he was working on his next movie and couldn't make the wedding, he wished them well.

They were having a big party for all their friends when they returned to London. Amanda and Pete couldn't go to the wedding as their youngest had chickenpox and Pam was due to give birth any day but hoped to be at the party. Tony was in his element; he loved Faith with all his heart and knew this was what was supposed to happen; he often wondered if the old Faith was watching, and of course, she was.

Months went by Tony and Faith were so happy with their new life together. Faith rented out her flat and lived at Tony's, this suited them well. It wasn't a big flat, but there was enough space for her things including her sofa that she loved. They had nights in and went out, they were often late for parties as Faith would get Tony to pull over suddenly and surprise Tony with surprise sex in the most unusual places. They were often nearly caught by passers-by and Tony decided if his wife continued to surprise him, he would have to get secrecy glass in his car. She didn't care, she was excited by the prospect of being caught, but there were laws against that kind of thing, so to allow her to do this often he got the glass. He loved that she was so spontaneous and daring! Of course, he loved having sex with her. Tony watched his wife like a hawk making sure his friends never gave her drinks, and he never found out who it was that spiked her drinks that night at the party but he made sure it never happened again.

Faith took modelling jobs when she felt like it, but found that she mostly had opportunities for tv commercials. She was enjoying her freedom to choose. She went out with Kate shopping for the new baby. She was quick to help out with Pete's and Bob's children at the drop of a hat. Everyone liked Faith, especially the children. Kate, Amanda and Pam were all at least ten years older than Faith, so they treated her like a little sister, they were very protective of her. Faith loved this as she had never had people in her life that cared so deeply about her; they were like one big family.

Ted and Kate had a beautiful baby boy, they called him Edward. It seemed to fit well, he had a shock of jet-black hair, the darkest brown eyes, and he had a little dimple on each cheek. He was a very calm baby, and he smiled every time he saw Faith. Of course, Faith made a huge fuss of him, making silly faces and cooing at him, she couldn't wait to have a baby of her own, but for now she had to make do with baby Edward. Before he was six months old, Kate was pregnant again which made Bob laugh. He thought he was bad having little gaps between his growing horde, Kate was happy as she didn't want big gaps between her children, but Faith still wasn't pregnant. She began to worry whether she could have children,

"Just relax baby it will happen when it happens." Tony would say, but this didn't help. Faith wanted children so badly. She kept herself busy with Pete's children and Bob's and now

Ted's. She read to them the *Adventures of Redwall* and *The Animals of Farthing Wood*. The children sat enthralled while Faith acted out the parts as she read, she read Edward the *Tales of Peter Rabbit* and *Flopsy Bunny* and *Mrs Tiggy Winkle*. She played pirates with the older children, they all loved Auntie Faith. Tony would film them all playing and the dramatics Faith got them all to do.

The months rolled by and Kate had another son, they called him Charles, "a very regal name" Faith said looking at the little scrap in the cradle, he was identical to his brother, so cute.

However, by this time Edward's hair had started to lighten up, he was a confident chap, still loved his Auntie Faith and was a little upset when she was holding the new baby and started to cry. "Oh, my little man," Faith said, "you are still my special buddy, come here and give me a hug." Edward looked at Faith as if he was waiting for her to put the baby down, she passed the baby to Tony and he ran to her, hugging her tightly, "oh dear I hope he will be okay when I have my baby." she said.

"What?" Everyone said in surprise.

"Yes, it's due in September" she said.

Tony looked very pleased with himself until Ted said "About time, I thought you were broken again."

They all laughed, Tony didn't think it was funny though. Faith was relieved too; she had started to think she wasn't going to fall at all. Maybe now Tony could rest as she couldn't possibly want so much sex while she was pregnant, how wrong he was, Faith's sex drive was insatiable.

Old Faith was sitting watching all the fuss, and she was glad that Ted had listened to her. He looked very happy with Kate, she looked glowing; she loved her little boys, and loved Ted more than ever, he was a doting father and husband and was surrounded by his family. His parents were proud of him and doted on their new grandsons, and his sister was always at their house helping with the children. Old Faith knew it was still a struggle for Ted as he denied his true feelings, but it was a small price to pay for his life, he would rather be alive and healthy. Kate took great care of Ted. He did love his Kate over anyone else in his life. They made the cutest couple. He was so proud of his sons and loved parading them about like little kings.

# Chapter Ten
## The new house

Faith was about five months pregnant when Tony took her on a drive, out to the Surrey countryside. The sun shone through the scattered clouds. "Where are we going?" she enquired.

"Oh, just for a little drive, we can have lunch at the Farmers Inn." he said.

"Sounds nice." she said. She didn't press him as he undoubtedly was planning something, he liked to surprise Faith, she just sat and enjoyed the countryside passing by. Finally, they got to a long driveway. "Oh, are we here?" she said looking around.

"Yes, just down here." There before them was a lovely big mansion.

"It looks like a hotel." she said.

"Well not quite. It's for sale, only six bedrooms and six acres of land," he said.

"Really? Can we afford this?", she said taking in the view.

"Yes, we can," he said proudly, "but if you don't like it, we can keep on looking."

"Let's have a look, shall we?" she said excitedly. He helped her out of the car. They knocked at the door, and a man with a suit opened the door.

"Good afternoon sir, madam." he said as Tony and Faith went inside. A man was coming down the stairs.

"Mr and Mrs Mathews, I presume?"

"Yes." Tony shook the man's hand.

"I'm David Peters I'll be showing you around today."

"Thank you." Tony said as they followed the man around the house. Tony took each room in, not saying much, as the man told them the details of each room.

Faith just followed looking around the huge house, she was more concerned with the bedrooms and the gardens, she had never seen such a big house. The parquet floors were beautiful, she loved the leaded windows, and the conservatory was bigger than their flat! She had also never seen so many bathrooms in one house, and the oak panelling was to die for. She was looking worried; Tony noticed,

"What's wrong darling? Don't you like it?" he said.

"I love it" she replied "but who is going to keep it clean?" Tony burst out laughing. "What?" she said "What's so funny?"

"We will have a housekeeper," he said trying to stop laughing.

"Oh," she said, feeling slightly silly.

"There is another building outside that I can use as a studio, and when we have parties it won't be in the main house disturbing the kids." he said. She liked that idea. If the studio were in the garden, Tony would be nearby most of the day, and the gardens were huge too. Faith imagined a huge greenhouse somewhere in the grounds where she could grow organic food. "So, what do you think Faith? Do you like it enough to live here?" Tony said.

"Where will I put my couch?"

Tony laughed again. "Anywhere you want Faith; you can have whatever you want, this will be our home," he said.

"Can we have a rowing boat on that lake?" she said pointing to the lake in the garden, to see if he meant it.

"Of course, can you row?" He said.

"Of course, I can, can't you?" she said.

"I'm sure I can," he said laughing.

Two months later they were ready to move into their new home. There wasn't much to look at as the flat was tiny and Tony wanted new furniture, the rooms looked empty and bare. Tony frowned, "This won't do," he said, "we shall have to go furniture shopping, or the house will look empty. What do you think about someone coming in and doing it all for us?" he said.

"I don't want someone else choosing for us." she said. "I really would like to do it ourselves." Faith said.

"Yes, but I don't have time, and you are pregnant, I don't want you lifting anything." Tony said.

"I won't, I promise." she said, "I'll get someone to deliver, and put things where I want them, then you can let me know what you think about things when you have time," she said. "Please let me do this Tony, I'm sure I can." she said.

He looked at her. "Okay, do one room at a time, you have to promise you won't overdo it okay." He said wrapping his arms around his wife. She smiled and buried her face into his shoulder. She loved how he smelled, she could stay there in the comfort of his arms all day and never be bored.

The next day Faith went to a few antique shops. She wanted the look to be perfect, she picked some large oak sideboards, a huge matching dining table and twenty chairs, a few knick-knack's, she found some cushions in the same sort of fabric as the curtains, and a chaise for between the two long windows. She had taken a sample of the curtain material and got the chairs recovered in a similar type of material, a shade darker than the curtains. She went to a carpet shop and bought a huge area rug for under the table, she was so excited to see the finished result.

Still, she had to wait a week for delivery. This gave her time to get the painters in. She chose contrasting colours and wallpaper, she then turned her attention to the small living room where she had decided her comfy sofa would live. There was enough room for another sofa, so she went in search of another either the same or similar. She chose the colours of the walls to go with her sofa and the painters got to work, she loved this decorating lark, and found she was really good at it, well she was good at picking the colours and fabrics as she had promised not to overexert herself. She had other people do the actual work and to be honest, she didn't think she would have done such a good job if she had to pick up a paintbrush.

She walked into another store in a long line of stores she had been to in just a week, and there it was, her sofa and two matching armchairs, she was so pleased with herself. She chose a large coffee table to go between the sofas and another rug, 'oh I do hope Tony likes it', she thought. Tony gave her cart blanch to do whatever she wanted, and even when he came home and saw what she had created he loved everything. They ended up spending a lot of time in the small living room as it was very comfortable, Faith slowly worked her magic on the rest of the house over the next month, she had done a fabulous job.

Tony wasn't sitting on his laurels either. Between time in the studio he had a huge greenhouse built on the quiet side of the garden, with underfloor heating put in it, and all the staging was completed before Faith noticed anything was going on over that side, she was so excited. The greenhouse was so big and warm she put a huge olive tree inside and on one side there was a deep raised bed where she put some grapevines, in red and white. There was even a drip-feed water system, so she didn't have to remember to water everything.

One morning a truck arrived at the gate. Tony went out to see what it was, "Delivery for Mrs Mathews." the driver said. He had two other men in the cab.

"What is it?" Tony asked.

"It's from a Prince Kasim, or something," he replied.

"Okay, bring it in." Tony opened the gates, it looked like a load of fences.

"Where do you want it?" the driver said.

"I don't know, how big is this present?" Tony was looking quite worried, he couldn't turn down a present from a Prince to his wife. The driver gave Tony the paperwork, it read:

"Dearest Faith, congratulations on your wedding. I know you loved my white peacocks when you were at the palace so I have selected four of my best for you. I have sent a pen so they can be safe and be sure not to let them out for six weeks as they may fly away. And then only let the females out as they are more social. I hope you have room for them. Best regards Prince Kasim."

Tony looked stunned 'peacocks?' "Okay, they had better go by the greenhouse." Tony pointed towards the other side of the garden. The men drove over the grass to the greenhouse and started to unload the pen and put it together. Faith noticed the movement down by her greenhouse and walked down to see what was happening. she saw the crates on the floor and looked inside, she jumped up and down with glee

"Oh Tony, they are beautiful how did you know I loved peacocks?"

"I didn't," he said "it's a gift from your Prince Kasim."

"He's not my Prince darling, you are." She jumped on his back kissing him on his neck, she never cared if people saw her acts of affection to her husband. As Tony never minded, she carried on.

The pen was huge and took up a lot of room, but Faith was so excited she had peacocks of her own, Tony thought they were nice to look at, but over the coming weeks realised how bloody noisy they were, but Faith was happy, so he didn't mention it to her.

# Chapter Eleven
## Company

Tony had decided to hold a house warming party for his friends, to show off his new house and his very pregnant wife. Faith got a catering company to provide the food and a bar. There were so many people there, Faith didn't know most of them, but luckily Kate and Amanda were there early, and Pam was close behind. Faith showed them around the house, then it was time for drinks in the kitchen where there was a debate going on about religion. Faith ducked out, "Sorry," she said, "I never talk about politics or religion." And she left the room, to the disgust of some of the guests.

"How rude!" she heard them say. This upset Faith immensely, she went to the conservatory for a breath of air as no one was in there. Tony saw the look on her face as she passed him and followed her,

"What's wrong baby, are you all right?" Faith stopped walking as she got to the conservatory.

"I think I've upset some of your friends," she said tearfully.

"Why? What happened?" He said putting his arm around her shoulders.

"I do my best never to talk about religion to anyone. It's boring, and no one has the same views, do they?" she said "they wanted me to join in the conversation. I'm sorry, I think maybe I was rude to them, I said I never talk about religion. But they seemed upset when I left the room. They didn't seem to like what I said."

"I think that everything wrong in the world could be down to religion, and money, wars, famine, everything." Tony smiled at her. "This is your house darling, if you don't want to talk about religion you don't have to, and they can go to hell."

"I don't believe in hell Tony." she said.

"What do you believe in Faith?", he said looking her in the eyes.

"I believe in the sun and the moon, and I believe in this," as she grabbed a handful of dirt from a pot plant. She touched her stomach and said, "I believe in this," as she stepped closer "and this" as she kissed him tenderly, "and Tony I believe in you. I don't believe in an invisible god that people worship, I believe in energy and everything is connected by an electrical life force. Apart from that force, I only believe what I can see. Its called life force energy, I'm sorry if people can't understand that, but it's how I feel, and I don't feel I have to explain to anyone."

He smiled again, "Sounds about right to me," he said, "I don't believe in God either, but I couldn't have put it that eloquently. I'm glad you don't rush off to church every Sunday, I just thought you were young and didn't go to church because you have better things to do," he said.

"I do have the things that I do", she said, "I like crystals." she said.

"What kind of crystals?" he asked

"Amethyst, obsidian, tiger's eye, that sort."

"Oh okay" he said.

"They have energies of their own, qualities that protect and make you strong," she said.

"Strong?" he questioned.

"Not in a physical way, in a spiritual way, although some people believe they make you physically strong." she said.

"oh okay." he nodded.

"That's why I wanted your hair." She took his hand and led him up the stairs to their bedroom. On her dresser was a wooden box, it was beautiful but simple, she opened it inside were crystals and something tied up with purple ribbon.

"What's that," he said pointing at the object.

"This is you and me." she said. "This is the hair you gave me and mine, and when our baby is old enough for a haircut, I will put that hair in with ours. This is our family and us, and these crystals are for protection, and our birthstones, mine is amethyst, and yours is this green one peridot, and onyx is for Leo too." she said. "Also, clear quartz and this one is rose quartz, Jasper and obsidian, all protection stones." As she was closing the box, he said he liked that thought.

"That is really sweet Faith," he said "I can see how this works for you." he said smiling, she smiled.

"I'm glad you don't think I'm a witch." she said laughing.

"Well" he said, "it is witchcraft though isn't it?"

"Yes," she said "but not in a bad way."

"I always wondered how you know what I think before I tell you," he said.

"That's just because I know you and know what you are like." she said. "I'm in tune with you, I like to please you, you give me so much Tony I couldn't be happier."

"We better go back to our guests," Tony said as he kissed her softly.

"Yes, we should," she said "I'm starving and the baby needs feeding too," she said as she walked back down the stairs.

Nearly everyone was talking about Faith and Tony in one way or another.

"Look at the way she leads him around" one person said.

"Talk about controlling!" another said.

"oh my god how sweet do they look together?" another person said.

"He looks so happy I've never seen him smile so much in a girlfriend's company."

"They are married I think," the other person said, "he's so attentive."

"She looks like she's about to burst, should she be here in that state?"

Ted overheard some not so kind comments and got a bit angry. "Don't you just love how they look together" he said very loudly to Kate, "I just love her so much."

"Yes," Kate agreed, "they are perfect for one another, I bet that baby is going to be gorgeous." she said even louder. She stopped and paused and looked at Ted saying, "Actually darling, I have something to tell you." Kate started to say a bit quieter.

Ted looked at her smiling, "what darling?" he said.

She continued "I don't know if this the place or not, I know we decided to just have the two, but I think we will have three."

"Three what? Darling." Ted turned to Kate

"Children, darling, I think I'm having another one" she said.

"Think or know dear?" he said looking slightly put out.

"Know" she said. Ted loved his children but still struggled with fatherhood, being woken up in the night and changing nappies wasn't his favourite pastimes. "Maybe this will be a girl" she said trying to appease him. He wasn't convinced and decided it was time to get drunk. Kate felt deflated when Faith bumped into her, as she gave her another drink.

"I know you're on the fruit juice" she said "here try this, no alcohol." she laughed, then saw Kates face, "what happened?" Faith said.

"I just told Ted I'm pregnant and he seemed annoyed." Kate said trying to hold back the tears

"It's just new that's all," Faith said "he doesn't mean to be insensitive I'm sure," she said making up her mind to give Ted a piece of her mind.

"I guess it's a bit soon after Charles, but it was an accident." Kate said.

"Yes, but it does take two to have one of those." Faith said slightly annoyed. "Don't worry Kate it will be fine, maybe this is a girl?" She smiled.

"I love my boys but really would love to have a little girl." Kate confessed.

"You are slightly outnumbered in your house" Faith agreed.

"It's not the end of the world," she said "is it?" Kate said weakly.

"Of course it isn't," Faith said, "I want more than three, and I'm sure Tony does too," she said. "I'm not sure I like parties," Faith said, looking around at the people in her house.

"Why? It's okay" said Kate.

"I've been to some parties, and people at those seemed a lot more polite." said Faith, "I just overheard someone saying they didn't like someone's dress! They aren't wearing it, so why would they have an opinion on that," Faith said.

"Really?" Kate said, "it wasn't my dress, was it?"

Faith laughed, "No it wasn't, and if it were, they would be blind, your dress is very nice," she said.

"Faith," Kate said, "nice is something someone says when it's hideous." They both laughed.

"I didn't know that!" Faith said going slightly red, "well I like your dress," she said.

"So do I," Kate said "that's why I wore it." They both laughed.

"I didn't think mine was going to fit this morning", Faith said truthfully, "I bought it weeks ago. I've grown," she said, laughing.

They were having such fun laughing at their own expense Ted came over to see what was so funny. Faith just looked at Ted and laughed again.

"You two look like you're having fun, what's in those glasses? I do hope no alcohol."

Faith nonchalantly said for him to mind his own business, Tony overheard her "I do hope that isn't alcohol darling." Faith and Kate stopped laughing.

"Of course not, it's just giggling juice" Faith said looking at Kate they started to laugh again.

Tony sipped from Faith's glass "mm, what is that? It's nice." he said.

"I mixed it for us, pregnant ladies," Faith said looking at Kate, "mango and papaya with passionfruit, and a little soda water makes it more like a cocktail doesn't it?" she said.

"Yes, very nice." he said giving Faith her glass back.

Faith decided to snag Ted's arm, "Come with me sir," she said dragging him to the other side of the room.

Tony stayed with Kate, "So you're having a baby?"

"Yes," Kate said "I don't think Ted is happy about it though."

Tony laughed. "He will get over it." he said.

"I hope so," she said.

Faith looked at Ted menacingly, "What are you doing?" she said.

"What do you mean darling?" he protested.

"I know it's a little soon after Charles, but it does take two to have a baby you know, and if you didn't want another you should have taken precautions." she said prodding his chest.

"Yes, yes I know Faith," he said backing away from Faith.

"She is over there devastated that you had an adverse reaction to the news you are having another child," she continued following him, "she loves you so much, and you act like she did something wrong. If you don't want any more, go sort yourself out" she said very quietly.

"What?" he said.

"You know" she whispered gesturing downwards.

He looked at her in horror, swallowing hard, "Don't you think that's a little harsh?" he said looking wounded.

"No, I don't," she said. "It's a small snip for a guy, but a huge operation for a woman, and if it's you who doesn't want any more, don't you think you should do the manly thing?" she said.

Ted loved Faith, he said "Who knew you were going to be so much trouble!" he said as he wrapped his arms around her, "I do see what you are saying Faith, and I will apologise immediately, but I'm not snipping anything from my extremities though." he laughed. He went back to his wife and hugged her tightly. "I'm sorry darling," he said kissing her "I love you very much, and if we are having another baby, I'm sure it will be as beautiful as the other two."

Kate buried her face in between his shoulder and neck, kissing him, "I'm sorry darling, I didn't mean to ruin the party for you."

He looked at her and said, "My darling wife, I love you to the moon and back nothing you could do would ruin anything in this world. Actually, come to think about it, it would be lovely to have a little girl, but this one better look like you." And they both laughed.

# Chapter Twelve
## Tour

Faith was due to give birth any day now and was hoping she had the baby before the band went on tour in October. Kate was packing her babies up and going with them. Faith was sure if Kate can do that she could too, even though she wanted to get her baby into a routine, she was sure it wouldn't matter if she were in a hotel or at home. Bob's wife Pamela always took their children along with a tutor, as the children were older, as were Pete's children. Amanda was an old hand at planning how she would cope with her brood while on tour. Faith wasn't worried at all as the wives made themselves available at a moment's notice. It would be all hands, on deck, as Faith helped them when they needed an extra hand with the children. They liked Faith a lot. They knew she liked them, and there was very little bickering between them. Luckily, they all had similar parenting styles, so all the children got along with each other and got treated the same. Faith was amazing with all of the children, and the other wives knew Faith would help them at a moment's notice also.

Kate said she was excited to go on tour as she hadn't been for two years and said she was going to keep Ted out of trouble. Still, they all knew she didn't like the separation for her boys and herself. Faith thought if Kate can do it so will I.

She could pack up the baby and go with Tony, the tours got easier for Tony as he knew exactly where his wife was.

He was excited to become a father and hoped he would be better than his father; he had a strict upbringing. He wouldn't be a strict father he knew that, and he worried how Faith would cope as she was so young. Still, Faith had everything she needed for her new baby, the nursery was beautiful, it was right next to the master bedroom. She made sure she had everything she needed to be on the road also.

They were hiring a nanny to come with them, they had carried out several interviews for the position and Faith set out what the requirements of the new nanny were. Faith would be the primary caregiver to her child, the nanny was only required in the evenings, when the baby had been put to bed so Faith could go to the shows with Tony, and when Faith needed a rest. She had already decided to do most things herself, she didn't have to clean the house or do laundry as they had hired a housekeeper, Mrs Simpson. She was a jolly middle-aged lady with rosy cheeks and a smile for everyone. It took Faith a long time to get used to having someone clean up after her, she liked things done her way, so the housekeeper had to be shown how Faith liked things to be done. Faith liked her home to be homely but also clean. They didn't have pets, so there was no pet hair or anything to clean up, but she liked her bedsheets to be changed daily, and vacuuming had to be done daily, the kitchen and bathrooms had to be immaculate at all times as they had guests often.

Old Faith was enjoying watching her life unfold, she couldn't wait to see her son's face, wondering whether he would take after Tony or her, or a mixture of both. She overheard them talking about a name if it was a girl, but of course, she knew it was a boy, so the name that they had picked was Drew Edward Mathews which had a nice ring to it, she thought.

Finally, the baby made his appearance on the first of October, they registered him, Drew Edward, after Ted. Everyone was excited to see him, the waiting room was full of Faith and Tony's friends. As Faith looked at her son lovingly his dark hair and pale skin, and the cutest button nose, Tony sat on the side of the bed looking in awe at the tiny baby, he was so happy that Faith didn't have too terrible a time giving birth, he was proud of the way she handled it all. Faith didn't want him to know how much pain she was in, but all was forgotten when she saw her son all pink and healthy, he had all his fingers and all of his toes.

Everyone came in one by one to see the new addition to the family. Kate had a nice cuddle, Ted was making jokes about him all in good humour. Once they got home from the hospital, they gave a huge sigh of relief, but it took a week to sort out all the gifts they had received and write thank you notes to everyone. Tony went to pick Faith's mother up to visit the new baby. She was more impressed at the huge house they lived in, she looked at the baby and smiled, but didn't want to hold him, and after dinner, Tony took her home.

When he returned Faith was in the lounge, she was very quiet, he asked Faith if she was alright, she burst into tears, "can we not do that again Tony," she cried, "I want nice people around our son, people who will show they love him, I don't want him to feel hurt by her indifference, grandparents are supposed to love their grandchildren aren't they?"

"I'm glad you said that Faith", he said, "I had no idea she could be so cold."

"I have tried to tell you before, but every time we have been there, she acted differently, so you didn't see it"

"Well now I know," he said, "luckily we are so busy, I don't like being like that openly." he said.

Faith often thought that her mother had a duel personality and often she would surprise Faith by not having the reaction that Faith expected, but this was the last straw, it was very personal. She resigned to keeping herself busy, especially as Christmas was coming up and it was her son's first.

Old Faith sat back tearfully as she recalled how her mother was. She wouldn't give her children the time of day unless they had blue eyes, it was strange, even when she did have a blue-eyed child Faith sometimes thought it would have been better if she didn't let her mother near her children at all, as she would tell them Faith didn't love them and other nasty things.

The tour had started, and Faith had to juggle taking care of her infant and being there for Tony. The travelling was difficult with such a small baby, but at least he wasn't crawling, and they would be at home by Christmas, then in the New Year the band would be going to America. Faith had decided not to go in January as the weather was very cold, and travelling around would be too uncomfortable. Tony had made sure that he held his son as often as possible. Before the shows they spent hours relaxing backstage as they spent all their energy on stage, he was usually exhausted after the shows, but while they were relaxing, he held little Drew all the time showing off to everyone, it was plain to see he was proud of his little boy.

Christmas came and went, Faith enjoyed decorating the house and they had the biggest tree she had ever seen. She had spent a fortune on decorations, and after Christmas, they planted the Christmas tree in the front of the house. Next year they would cover it in lights. Faith loved Christmas, they had bushes of holly and even had some mistletoe growing in some of the trees in their garden, she hand-made all the centrepieces to go on the table all held together with ivy. They had all their friends over for dinner on Boxing Day. Tony's parents came for the weekend, they were so pleased with their grandson. They made a fuss of him at every opportunity. Tony was glad they didn't disappoint him as Faith's mother had. His father was quite a strict parent when he was young, but with the baby, he saw a side of his father he had never seen, it made him smile.

Just as they were taking down the decorations from Christmas it was almost time for the new tour to start. Faith wasn't feeling very well, Tony lay on the bed with her and Drew.

"How are you feeling Faith?" he said kissing her hand.

"I'm feeling really tired and a little sick" she replied, "I hope it's not a bug, I wouldn't want Drew or you to catch it."

"Shall I take him downstairs?" he asked. Faith hated giving her son to the nanny to take care of as he fussed when she was near him.

"Actually, darling I'm not sure about this nanny he doesn't seem to like her at all, he never cries when he's with me, but when he's with her he cries all the time, she doesn't seem to be able to settle him", she said.

Tony looked at his wife. "That's why I brought him upstairs, she couldn't stop him crying, does he need changing"?

Faith took his nappy off, he had a pinch mark on his thigh, "what's this?" she said showing Tony

"I don't know," he said, "he didn't have that when I changed him this morning."

Faith looked at the mark closely. "Someone has pinched him." she said angrily.

"Well I didn't" he said sharply

"That leaves only one person, am I overreacting?" She said.

"If she is hurting our son she needs to go, that's why he doesn't like her."

Tony got up and left the room.

"Where are you going?" she called after him, she wasn't feeling up to getting up to see. She heard shouting from downstairs. The housekeeper came upstairs to sit with Faith, she looked quite scared.

"What's going on," she said to Faith.

"I think the nanny has pinched Drew on his leg," Faith said, as she showed the housekeeper the pinch mark.

"Oh, poor thing," she said almost crying. "Why would anyone do such a thing?" she said.

"I have no idea. Still, she is going." Faith said.

"Yes, that's what Tony was saying to her, she was trying to say she hadn't done anything to him. But to be honest, I thought she was a little rough with him yesterday."

Faith looked at the housekeeper. "Why didn't you tell me?" she said.

"I thought I was seeing things, I didn't want to cause any trouble. My eyes aren't what they were," she said. "I'm so sorry I should have said."

Tony reappeared into the room looking like thunder, Faith looked at him,

"Is she going?" she said expectantly.

"Yes, she is she's packing her stuff now," he said.

"I had better check she doesn't take anything that's not hers," the housekeeper said rushing out of the room.

Faith was clutching her son brushing his hair with her fingers, as he was cooing away.

"Poor thing." Faith said, "I hired that horrible woman, I feel terrible."

Tony took her hand and kissed it. "You weren't to know, it's a minefield getting a good nanny. I suppose I should contact her agency and tell them why I've sacked her, make sure they don't give her another job looking after someone else's baby." he said.

"I'm not sure I want someone else either, what if the next nanny is the same?" she said.

"I don't know darling, can you look after Drew by yourself?" he said.

"Of course I can." she answered.

"But I won't be here next week," he said.

"I have the housekeeper, she can do all the cleaning," Faith said laughing "people do look after their children you know," she said still brushing her fingers through her son's hair, he was asleep now.

"Yes, but you aren't feeling well either," Tony said.

Faith laughed "I'm not dying Tony I'll be okay. I'll go to the doctor's tomorrow and get something to make my stomach settle, and I'll sleep when he does." she said.

"Maybe I should get some help for Mrs Simpson?" he said.

"That might be a better idea," Faith said, "she can be the boss though," she laughed.

The following day Faith went to the doctor. The doctor looked at her sternly, "Mrs Mathews I believe you could be pregnant." he said.

Faith went pale. "Are you sure?" she said.

"No, I'm not," he said "you should have a test."

Faith arranged a test for the following morning; she didn't know how to tell Tony, Drew was only three months old, would he have the same reaction as Ted?

# Chapter Thirteen
## Joy

She found out a few days later that she was pregnant, so she plucked up the courage to tell Tony. She found him in the studio, "What's up darling?" he said as he embraced her playfully.

"I've been to the doctors." she said "I'm pregnant."

Tony looked at her to see if she was joking, she wasn't, "Are you okay with that?" he said.

"I'm fine, but I was a little worried how you would take it." she confessed.

"I'm okay with it, we didn't just want one baby, did we?" he said. "I am away in six days for a month, will you be okay?"

"I'm sure I'll be fine darling," she said hugging him.

"Well that's all right then," he said smiling and playfully kissing her neck. "We will have to sort that extra help out as soon as possible then." he said. She agreed. As she turned to go back to the house, he slapped her on the backside, she turned around as though she was going to get him back. However, she just laughed and went back to the house; she phoned Kate, a little shocked still, Kate laughed.

"Do you want me to come over tomorrow, we can have a good natter."

"Yes, that would be lovely, shall I bring Pamela and Amanda we can make a day of it?" Kate was eight months pregnant by this time, so the company was welcome.

"I'll ask Tony if he minds, as that works out to be a lot of kids running about." she laughed.

"Well mine won't be running about," she said, "yes, but with Pamela's three and Amanda's three, I'm sure it will be fine. I turned the games room into a playroom, if you tell them to bring some toys, I don't have any their age range yet." she said.

Tony didn't mind at all as he liked it when all the girls got together, anything that made Faith happy, made him happy. Over the coming weeks, Faith had the girls over every Tuesday and Thursday; she bought some slides and trikes for the children to play with while the mums nattered. Mrs Simpson and the new housemaid, Tilly, laid out food for the children and when they had a bit of time, playing board games with the older children. Amanda and Pamela loved helping with the new babies, and Kate and Faith helped with the older ones, Faith loved reading and playing pirates with the children.

In no time at all Tony and the boys were back from the tour, they stayed in the studio at home until Kate and Faith produced their babies. Kate had a little girl, she called her Faith Marie, she was just like the boys, but her eyes were lighter hazel.

Later that same year Faith had a boy, Gage Antony, he was blonder than Drew was at birth, but now Drew's hair was almost white, and his eyes were piercing blue. Tony doted over his boys, helping whenever he could between writing and recording. The families were always together; it was like a huge commune at Tony and Faith's house. It was a happy place, there was always something going on, Faith was very happy with her lot in life, her beautiful family and friends.

Ted was happy too, he still thought of the day Faith came into his life and turned it upside down. Obviously young Faith had no idea, but old Faith was always watching, she loved seeing herself in such a different role, watching how she managed her home and growing family.

Faith grew her organic food and turned it into baby food, and all the girls loved Faith's vegetable soup as the winters were very cold and it really helped when they ate the soup with homemade bread all organic, of course.

Her beautiful peacocks served as very good bug patrol too, Faith had planted fruit trees in the paddock, and this helped give the children a more healthy diet, everyone thought that Faith should start her own line of baby food, but she couldn't be bothered she was too busy with everything else she needed to do.

It was over a year later Faith fell for her third baby after they had a skiing holiday. She was elated to find out she was having another baby and hoped it was a girl. However, it wasn't, she had another boy, Jude Peter, he arrived in late February it was still cold outside, he was a quiet baby. Faith worried about him a lot, she couldn't understand why he didn't cry much. She took him to the doctors and asked for a hearing test as she heard babies that don't cry a lot were usually deaf, but he was perfect, nothing wrong he was just a quiet baby, and the other two boys were growing like weeds.

It was time Tony went on tour again, this time Faith decided to go with him, they had their boys one each side in the plane and the baby in the middle; Tony looked after Drew and Faith had Gage, and they shared the little one. It was lovely to see how they worked together looking after their boys, and luckily the children were very good, never seemed to fight or have tantrums.

Faith loved her growing family so much, Tony was everything to her; they never seemed to tire of each other's company. Faith's changeable personality and spontaneity kept Tony on his toes, and Tony's fun-loving side kept Faith interested. She was seldom bored and always busy either with her boys or the house and garden when Tony was away. Faith didn't like going on tour when it was winter, she hated the cold, but the weather was nice in Japan so all the girls went. They were all learning to speak Japanese. The boys could already speak a little as they had been to Japan several times, Ted was especially good at picking up languages, but Kate was catching up fast, Faith was hopeless but very funny as she copied the tapes she put on a gruff voice pretending she was a samurai and pulling faces she had everyone in stitches, it was very funny.

Before she came into their lives they argued incessantly about lyrics and music and even whose turn it was to make coffee, but Tony couldn't remember the last row they had -- he hadn't smashed anything in ages, it didn't hinder their artistic talent, their songs were really strong and the band was becoming world famous. It was like alchemy, they blended and moulded everything into their art, they never seemed to be arrogant or think they were better than anyone else, except Ted. He knew they were better than other bands, but they were well liked by other musicians, probably because Ted was the most talented musician alive. Bands were lining up to support them. They were always polite and kind and they made so many friends along the way. The girls were very tight, the best of friends.

Pamela had to go home half way through the tour as she became very ill, it turned out she was pregnant with twins. Bob wanted to go with her, but he had to stay so Amanda went with her instead to look after the children and supported Pam. Faith didn't want to leave Tony, so she stayed, and Kate stayed with her. They always supported each other during tours. When the tour was over, they went home, and Pam got better too, it seemed her babies didn't like Japanese food.

Faith had seen a sandpit while she was touring, it had a huge galleon in the middle. She asked Tony if they should have one in their garden as the boys would love that as they got older, he agreed, he loved that Faith wasn't demanding.

Still, she did know what she liked, and he didn't feel anything she had asked for was out of the realms of possibilities or spending silly amounts of money. Their home was full of tasteful furniture and accessories always clean and warm. There were no children's toys all over the house like he had seen in his friends' houses. His children were not at all like other people's children, they didn't fight or argue, they didn't have tantrums, there wasn't a competition between them either, they shared everything even their mother who gave them all her time. She put them to bed every night reading stories and singing lovely soft songs.

Faith commissioned the sandpit, the galleon was made of the toughest timbers, it had a rock climbing walls, ladders, slides and rope climbing nets. The sandpit was huge, there was a small shed at the back so they could store the buckets and spades and all manner of toys to play in the sand, the ship had a steering wheel and a talking tube. Tony came home from a show he was doing in London to see the finished sandpit, he was shocked at the size of it but was impressed to see Faith standing on the deck dressed in her pirate garb whilst all the kids were running around shouting 'oooo arrr', he couldn't help but smile.

All the children loved playing in the sand and climbing all over the galleon, and the smaller ones just sat in the sand, filling up buckets, with their mothers.

Jude was two by the time Faith had her next child, finally a girl, Marisa Kate. She was dark like Drew at birth, but just like Drew her hair turned almost white as she got older and was curly as it got longer. Tony and Faith decided not to have any more children as they had three beautiful boys and the prettiest girl they had ever seen. He decided to go for a vasectomy. Ted was so shocked that Tony would do this as the thought of anyone chopping his privates scared Ted half to death. Tony was very uncomfortable for a week, but Faith took great care of him, running him hot salt baths whenever he felt in too much pain. Unfortunately, they were not told the vasectomy wasn't instant, and Faith fell pregnant again. They were in total shock, the doctor laughed and said: "It doesn't work instantly, you still have to take precautions for at least a month after."

Faith knew this pregnancy wasn't the same as the others, she felt very different; she grew faster. She thought it was her age, but she soon discovered she was having twins. Tony was really surprised but knew Faith would be fine. He was there all the time during this pregnancy and Faith rested well. Instead of walking around the garden, she had a treadmill so she could get off when she was tired and rest immediately. She didn't have to walk back to the house; she could still manage a bit of yoga and meditated every day for at least twenty minutes. She started showing her children how to do yoga; it was hilarious watching the children roll around the floor. Faith had quiet time with the older boys. They did a bit of meditation as the baby went to sleep with a pillow on the floor with her brothers. Faith showed the children how to picture things they wanted, and how to feel grateful for everything they had and be grateful that they had a good life, even Tony joined in, the whole house was calm and serene.

Faith gave birth to two beautiful girls, in the spring of her twenty-eighth year, at last, her family was complete. Elizabeth Amanda was the older twin, then came Eleanor Pamela. Bob was very upset, he thought they could of at least had a boy as he was the only one who didn't have one of Tony's children named after him.

"Okay, you can be the godfather of all of them," Tony said, laughing. This made Bob happy as he got all of the golden children. This was what they had started to call Tony's children as they all turned out blond, the twin's eyes were grey-green, but the others were all blue, a beautiful family.

The walls were adorned with pictures of their growing family, taken of course by Sophie, who was a world-renowned photographer, by this time, and was a constant visitor to their home. The house was full of laughter and happiness; they always had friends over for barbeques in the summer. Faith would organise huge parties on the equinoxes. The summer was especially good as it was all outside, they had bands playing music all day, and food and drink on tap, everyone dressed in their fanciest clothes. Faith and Tony had decided to build a huge L shaped barn with huge fireplaces at each end. With windows all down one side that could be open or closed, and with bi-folding doors at the front, with a bar at the back, and a large stage for the bands to play and the longest feasting table. The décor was very Pagan, and lots of their friends turned out to have the same views as them.

# Chapter Fourteen
## The calm, the storm

Tony and Faith danced through the months and the years of their perfect life, seldom argued and took great care of their growing brood. Drew and Gage were learning to play several instruments; piano, drums and both base and lead guitars. Jude had the voice of an angel as did Marisa. The boys adored their little sisters, the girls were so beautiful they were photographed wherever they went; all the children went to private school alongside some very prestigious people's children.

Faith took them everywhere with her when she modelled for major magazines. The children modelled too, but their hearts were in music, even Faith joined in some charitable recordings, she loved music from every genre including classical music. Still, her real passion was heavy rock. She got to meet every band she liked as she had a hall pass, being the wife of one of the most famous drummers in the world, he didn't mind that everyone fell for his wife's charms as he got to take her home. She never looked at any man the way she looked at him, he could be on the other side of the room, and he could feel her eyes would be on him and only him. She loved him so much no one ever made a play for her as she was quite clear who she was with.

While Tony was on tour without his Faith, he was propositioned by one of the beautiful fans, this wasn't unusual, but Tony was missing his wife, and took solace in the woman's arms. He didn't have sex with her, but it did come close. When he turned her down, she became violent, as she was very drunk, screaming at Tony that he would regret turning her down. Tony went back to his hotel room a bit shaken by the experience; he phoned his home number but there was no answer as Faith was in the garden playing with the children and the housekeeper was shopping. He drank half the minibar and fell asleep; he woke up to find the woman had managed to get into his room and was naked beside him. He jumped out of bed and ran to the bathroom yelling at her to get the hell out of his room. She didn't go. He came out of the bathroom with a robe on and called security, who promptly took her away.

That morning he and Ted had breakfast and talked about the crazy woman, this wasn't unusual in the old days, but Tony was over forty, he was happily married with six children. He would never cheat on Faith. What he didn't know was that the woman had taken pictures of him passed out naked on his bed, then took pictures of herself next to him and carefully put the pictures in her coat pocket before going to sleep beside him. She proceeded to sell the pictures to the press; it was front-page news. Tony had been a naughty boy.

Tony looked in horror at the front page of his newspaper; he knew he only had a few hours to get to Faith. He got on the first available flight home. Ted went with him; he had to do something or lose his family. He cut the tour short he told Pete and Bob to do the damage control.

Faith was in shock, her face went all numb as she sat looking at the newspaper.

"What are you looking at?" Kate said. Kate had been staying at the house with Faith on one of their girly dates; Faith showed her the newspaper. Kate didn't know what to say other than, "It's a fake, Faith, it isn't him."

Faith knew it was Tony; she couldn't imagine what had happened to make him cheat on her; she never turned him down, ever, why would he go with such a bimbo? She was very upset but she knew she had to put on a brave face for her children. She couldn't imagine living without her Tony, she didn't want to think about it, her mind went blank she just didn't know what to do. She hid how she was feeling all day from her children and Kate, but Kate knew something was going on in Faith's head.

"What are you going to do?" she asked.

"I don't know," Faith said numbly. "I guess I'll have to wait for him to come home, that is, if he does come home." When she had put the children to bed that night, she poured herself a large drink and downed it.

"Are you sure that's wise Faith?" Kate said, trying not to judge.

"What am I supposed to do Kate, huh? Tell me!" Faith snapped. "I'm so sorry," she said instantly, "I didn't mean it; it's not your fault at all, you are my dearest friend."

Kate sat down next to Faith and put her arm around her, as Faith tried hard not to have a meltdown.

"I know you are upset, but I honestly don't think that's what happened Faith. I don't. Tony hasn't looked at another woman since he met you, you remember how long ago that was? I know how he suffered when he couldn't have you, he waited. He has never waited for anything in all the time I've known him."

Faith was still thinking, she couldn't understand how this had happened. The phone rang and Mrs Simpson answered. She spoke very quietly and then she offered the phone to Faith, Faith declined. Kate took the phone, she just said "not now" and hung up the phone, it rang again, they ignored it, this time.

Tony was at Heathrow, he had to get home.

When Kate had gone to bed, Faith walked down to the studio, she was very drunk by this time, opening the door she looked around at the guitars and drum sets. She grabbed the closest guitar and swung it into the drums, smashing everything in her reach, the tears streamed down her face, as she screamed at the top of her voice.

After smashing everything up, she went into the sound room there was some cord belonging to an old microphone, on the floor. She swung the chairs into the glass partition smashing it, she tied the cord around her neck and looped it on a coat hanger on the wall, and dropped.

Old Faith screamed, "NO!" she looked around for Tony. He had just reached the front door she screamed at him, "The studio, Tony the studio!"

Somehow, he heard her and ran to the studio. He rushed into the door and saw the carnage. As he did the cord around Faith's neck snapped and she fell to the floor into the glass. He grabbed her lifeless body. He was screaming as he undid the cord "No! No! No! Faith My Faith. Please don't be dead! Baby. Please! Please! Don't! Don't!" Her face was covered in blood, as were her arms.

Ted came into the room and dragged Faith clear of the glass. He lay her on the grass outside and started CPR. "Go and get an ambulance Tony!" he shouted. Tony went back into the studio, but the phone was smashed. He ran to the house and called 999, then immediately returned to Ted.

He fell to the floor beside Faith crying like a baby. "I did this," he said, unable to breathe. He choked and coughed just as Faith took a breath. Tony grabbed her "Baby, my baby!" he cried.

She tried to get away from him, hitting him as hard as she could. He was saying sorry all the while. He picked her up and carried her to the house. He lay her on the sofa. Ted and Kate went to the kitchen to get some towels to try to clean her up, luckily there was no glass in her arms or her face.

"Let me die." Faith said weakly.

"Never!" Tony said, holding her hand as he always did.

The housekeeper let the paramedics in, and they took over, lifting Faith on to the stretcher and into the ambulance, Tony and Ted went too.

Ted, all the time, was relaying to Faith what had actually happened. She started to cry, "I'm sorry about your stuff, Tony. I'm so sorry it's all smashed."

Tony looked at Faith. "Do you think I care about any of that stuff Faith? You are the most important thing in my life! Faith those things can be replaced; you can't. I can't say sorry enough." he said. "This was all my fault, I should never have encouraged her, I was drunk and being silly, I never intended to let it go that far."

They got to the hospital.

After the doctor looked Faith over, and had her wounds dressed, he discharged her saying she needed some therapy. "She's not mad," Tony said protectively.

"She just tried to kill herself, Mr Mathews, you should wonder if she is safe to look after children in that state of mind,

I'm referring her to a therapist, please think about it." The doctor said, looking over his glasses at Faith.

Old Faith was looking on waiting for him to tell the doctor to go to hell; she knew why Faith did that but didn't dare say it even to herself. It wasn't about her; it was about her children; she didn't want him to leave them even if he left her.

Tony held on to his wife all the way home. Ted and Kate stayed in the guest suite so that they were there for Faith and Tony in the morning. Tony helped Faith get into bed then got in beside her, he wanted to find out what she was thinking too.

"Why Faith? You love the kids, don't you?"

"Yes," she said, "I love them more than life."

"Then why would you want to go away from them?"

"I thought you had left me, Tony you may leave me at any time, but you will not leave our children. I would rather let them have you alone than me alone." she said.

"What! I'm not leaving you, Faith, I would never leave you," he said.

"I didn't know that," she said, "I saw that picture, I knew it was you even though Kate said it wasn't. I knew it was, you have never been in that position unwillingly," she said.

He looked down, ashamed. "I'm so sorry Faith, I'm such an idiot. I knew I had to get home as soon as I saw that newspaper. I knew you would think I had left you. I don't know why you feel as though you just borrowed me. I don't know how to make you see you are the only one I want or need, without you I have no hand to hold, without you I can't breathe. You are everything to me, the kids are everything to me, I couldn't be prouder of you for raising the best kids I have ever met. I'm their dad, they love me. You love me, you always know what to say to me, but you never believe that I love you, why?" Tony asked.

"I don't know," she said looking away, "I'm ashamed of what I tried to do, I will never do it again." she said.

"Promise me," Tony said holding on to her hand.

"I promise," she said. She meant it, she almost ruined eight people's lives that night, her children would have never got over the fact their mother killed herself, all she had thought of was that he had left her and life wasn't worth living without him. But she was wrong about everything, he did love her and would always love her, she had to put her insecurities away for good. She thought she wasn't good enough for him, she had always thought that, she could never really get her head around the fact he thought she was amazing, even though she thought she was quite ordinary, no one else seemed to think that of her.

Over the next week Ted and Tony stayed close to Faith and Kate. Pete and Bob came back to England, the tour wasn't too much of a bust, they only had to cancel two shows. They didn't lose much money and gave the people tickets to the next show to compensate for the missed shows.

Faith had a small mark around her neck, but it went away in less than a month. As she got stronger Ted and Kate decided it was time to go home to their own house, but came over once a week to make sure Faith was okay and Tony wasn't driving her mad. He had been shopping for new drums and guitars and had the studio fixed up. It looked like nothing ever happened there. Still, Faith couldn't go in there for a long time, Tony didn't push her, even though he wanted her to make some backing tracks on their next album. He loved her voice, but had to make do with listening to her sing to the children.

She went to see a psychologist. They talked for a short time and Faith looked at her and said "I know what I did was stupid and really selfish, but I really don't think you can help me as I already know why I did that, I just need my husband." she said.

The therapist said "Why do you think you need him Faith?"

Faith thought for a while before answering. "We have a family, I have had a good life and the best times of that life was spent with my husband and children" she said, "we are a unit, we have a few really good friends that would do almost anything for us. My husband is amazing."

"Do you argue?" she said looking at Faith

"Define argue. We don't shout and scream at each other and throw things." she said honestly. "We don't always agree with each other." Faith said, "we discuss what we want and decide what's best."

"And who decides what is best Faith?"

"We both do, it depends on how important the outcome is, I usually decide what's best for our children, only based on if he is at home, we have rules in our house we all live by and I would never do anything to hurt or upset any one of my family members, we respect each other." she said.

"Are your children afraid of your husband?" the therapist said.

"No, why would they be afraid of him? He would never hurt them, he loves them."

"What about you Faith?" Faith looked at the woman who was asking stupid questions.

"I'm not afraid of him, he would never hurt me, I don't think he's ever raised his voice to me let alone hit me. What are you trying to ask me?" Faith said slightly annoyed, "I'm not a battered wife if that's what you think, and I'm not mentally or physically abused, apart from what I say to myself, that's my issues," she said. "Tony looks after me, he has never, or would ever, treat me badly."

She got up putting her coat on. "Send me the bill, I think this conversation is over." and left the room.

Over the next few weeks Tony and Faith were inseparable, they stayed at home most of the time looking after the children and taking the eldest children to school. Tony wrote a lot of really good material, the band spent a lot of time in Tony's new studio and the wives went shopping and had days out with the children, everything was back to normal as though nothing had happened.

Old Faith was exhausted, she sat back on her sofa feeling very tired. The woman looked at her and closed her eyes, Faith said "I think I will sleep now," as she closed her eyes, she smiled, it seemed a long time since she slept, she was happy at last.

Ted's sons grew into fine young men. Edward was very musically-minded but decided to go into law, and Charles went into the police force. He eventually headed MI5. Little Faith ran a management team. She managed some of the most prestigious bands of the new century, she had an eye for the next up and coming sounds.

Pete's and Bob's children did well in their lives too, going into law and they ran successful businesses. Tony and Faith's children were all very successful in the music business, and modelling world: Drew and Gage had a very successful rock band known the world over. Jude and the girls followed their mother into acting although Faith only did advertising. The children found their way into films, they rubbed shoulders with the elite, they each found their niche.

The families always got together on the summer solstice and of course Christmas, (or Yule, as Faith called it). They all had the charities they supported and led very busy lives, but they were never too busy for each other.

Ted, Kate, Tony and Faith were very proud of their families, and the rest of their family. Their brothers Pete and Bob along with Pamela and Amanda had never got on so well, writing songs wasn't such a fight, the egos weren't so apparent, even though Pete had projects he was doing with other bands.

Tony also had projects, they helped each other on their different projects, and always got together to write for the band they had all started so many years ago. They would continue into their old age as they had never lost popularity. They always sold out venues, the wives followed their husbands wherever they went and supported everything they did, and remained the best of friends till the end of their days.